PRAISE FOR MAILBOAT II
THE SILVER HELM

"Great job!... I can't wait for Mailboat III now!"
~ Lt. Ed Gritzner, City of Lake Geneva Police Department

"I finished Mailboat Book Two *in a matter of hours and as with* Mailboat Book One, *I found myself saying out loud as I read the last page, 'THIS CAN'T BE THE END!' You are a magnificent writer and leave your readers wishing the book's ending wasn't so soon. I found myself reading faster as I reached the middle of the story to find out what was going to happen next. Your readers are eagerly waiting for this story to be continued and you do not disappoint!"*
~ Lynda Fergus, author of the Lake House Lyn blog

"I finished it in one sitting! I loved it. I found myself readily identifying with each and every character. Well written, well 'fleshed out.' I just didn't want it to end... I want the WHOLE story. The answers to all this mystery! I wait impatiently for book 3!"
~ Kathy Collins

Danielle Lincoln Hanna

MAILBOAT

The Silver Helm

HHP

HEARTH & HOMICIDE PRESS, LLC
MISSOULA, MT
2018

Cover photography by Danielle Lincoln Hanna

Cover design by MaryDes
MaryDes.eu
With the contribution of Sandi Hanna Anderson

ISBN 978-1-7330813-2-0

BOOKS BY DANIELLE LINCOLN HANNA

The Mailboat Suspense Series

Mailboat I: The End of the Pier
Mailboat II: The Silver Helm
Mailboat III: The Captain's Tale
Mailboat IV - *coming summer 2020*

DanielleLincolnHanna.com/shopnow

JOIN THE CREW

Ahoy, Shipmate!

If you feel like you're perched on a lighthouse, scanning the horizon for Danielle Lincoln Hanna's next book—good news! You can subscribe to her email newsletter and read a regular ship's log of her writing progress. Better yet, dive deep into the life of the author, hear the scuttlebutt from her personal adventures, spy on her writing process, and catch a rare glimpse of dangerous sea monsters—better known as her pets, Fergus the cat and Angel the German Shepherd.

It's like a message in a bottle washed ashore. All you have to do is open it...

DanielleLincolnHanna.com/newsletter

MAILBOAT

SATURDAY
JUNE 21, 2014

CHAPTER ONE
BAILEY

It was too late at night for the lights to be on so bright. But there weren't any windows in the small, gray-walled room with the gray-topped table, so I guess it may as well have been noon or morning, or whatever time you like. Not midnight, though.

It was midnight. Maybe I should have said that first.

The light, white like mounds of ice stuck to the walls of a deep freezer, came from fluorescent bulbs, row-on-row in the ceiling.

The woman with the long, dark ponytail paced up and down, rubbing one temple distractedly as if she were talking to herself, not me.

"One more time, Bailey. Close your eyes. Try to picture him."

The killer. I closed my eyes, like the detective said. But instead of the murderer, I saw a man with wavy hair lying in the street. Riddled with bullets. Fighting to breathe. Moments before, he had chatted me up at the restaurant and learned all my hopes and dreams for when I graduated high school, when I went to college, when I had a life. He'd left me a hundred-dollar tip for no reason whatsoever. Maybe to put toward my college fund.

I'd seen him killed. I'd seen him die. His eyes were fixed. Calm. Eternal. Like two deep lakes staring forever into the stars.

Hot tears welled behind my eyelids. I crushed the hem of my tee shirt in my fist. But it wasn't my tee shirt. It had sharp fold lines and it smelled sweet and crisp, like cotton that's never been washed before. The detective had taken my own clothes away and sealed them in paper bags. They were covered in blood. The blood of the man with the wavy hair.

I bit my lip and told the dead man to leave me alone. I told myself to open my eyes and quit remembering him. But I couldn't do it. I couldn't look away. A single tear escaped and seared a line down my cheek.

Nylon squeaked, like the cords of a rope binding against each other. The sound of a man adjusting his seat while encased in a duty belt and bullet-proof vest. "Bailey?"

Ryan Brandt had been sitting in the corner in silence, letting the lady ask the questions. I didn't know why any of us had to be here. Why any of this had to happen. Why I had to be in the middle of it. I was exhausted. Not like when you've put in a long, hard day, or stayed up too late reading. I'd been reliving the shooting all night, aloud to the detective, and silently in my mind. I was sick-exhausted. My heart wanted to roll over and die.

"It's okay, Bailey," the woman said, with the closest impression of empathy her voice could muster. She didn't strike me as a very empathetic person. She wanted me to hurry the hell up and conjure a description of the murderer.

But all I could see was a world bogged in darkness. The kind that clings to your skin, dripping and cold, like slime. Like the slime of something dead and decaying. Something that was once flesh and muscle, but now only holds

3

together like the gooey remains of an overcooked vegetable. I saw darkness, and no way to escape it.

Except to go inside. Deep inside. My secret world. The place I called "make believe" when I was little. The place I now called "survival." It was where I went when I felt trapped in my foster home, when my foster dad was yelling at me, thrashing me, forcing me...

"What do you see?" the woman asked.

She thought I was still trying to remember the killer. But her voice sounded miles away. I was sinking deep into my own world, where I created my own realities, where I felt safe. My brain quit whirling and dodging as I entered a world no less crazy, but at least a world I controlled.

I imagined a room. Spartan, like this one, but cloaked in darkness. A flickering light bulb clung to a rusted circle of tin. I saw a man, pacing the floor, like the detective did. But he was old and balding and fat. His face was pasty, his eyes too close together, his nose small and hooked. The black leather holster on his chest contrasted with the whiteness of his shirt. He spoke with a thick accent.

"You still resist, comrade? Perhaps we have been too lenient on you."

Another man slumped in a chair, like the chair I was in, a chair in front of a gray-topped table. Only, his wrists were handcuffed behind his back. Behind the chair. His head hung low and his shoulders heaved with every breath.

I couldn't see the prisoner's face, but his hair was wavy and dark. I had never pictured him with dark, wavy hair before. The hero in my daydreams usually took on the form of some movie actor, or a character in whatever book I'd been reading. But sometimes, he looked like some random man I'd seen in the street or at work. In that regard, this latest incarnation wasn't so different from any of the ones who'd gone before.

"I don't care what you do to me," he rasped. *"I have nothing to tell you."*

"Is that so?" The man with the pasty face sneered. *"We have ways, you know."*

The prisoner lifted his head. His face was bruised and bleeding from a cut lip. *"Kill me now. Save yourself some time."*

The fat man didn't reply. He reached into his shirt pocket. Pulled out a scrap of glossy paper. Tossed it down on the table in front of the prisoner. It spun to a cock-eyed stop. The prisoner stared. It was a photo of a girl with wispy, brown hair—wavy like his own. Stubbornly uncontrollable like mine. It *was* mine. It was me.

"We know where to find her," the fat man said matter-of-factly.

The prisoner met the interrogator's eyes but maintained a perfect poker face as if the news meant nothing to him. Then with no warning, he sprang to his feet, grabbed his chair in his cuffed hands, whirled, and struck his captor. Wood splintered. The remains of the chair scattered. The fat man went down, crashing into the table. Half-dazed, he reached for his gun. A high kick from the wavy-haired man broke the interrogator's arm. The gun dropped to the floor. The interrogator crumpled to his knees, grasping his injury. One more kick laid him flat on the ground, unconscious, bleeding from the temple.

The man with the wavy hair stood over him, panting. He kicked the gun away, then knelt and fished in the agent's pocket for the keys to the cuffs. He let himself loose, then retrieved the firearm. He glanced toward the door. The guards would be here any minute. This was all happening prematurely. His plans weren't fully ready. But there was no turning back now.

He grabbed the photo of his daughter.

He was going home.

"Bailey?"

The voice of the ponytailed detective broke the reverie, just as the man with the wavy hair was slipping out of the interrogation room, shooting down Communist agents, fighting his way toward the outskirts of the compound and the razor-wired fence... fighting his way back to me.

"Can you picture him?" she asked.

Vividly.

She meant the killer, didn't she? I didn't care. I wasn't done daydreaming yet.

I'd never known my real dad. All my life, this was what I'd had for stand-ins: imaginary fathers. Sometimes they were captured secret agents, like this one. Sometimes they were in prison, serving a life sentence for a crime they'd never committed. Or they were prisoners of war, or of some remote, cannibalistic tribe. Or they were marooned on an island, or a maze-like jungle, or a desert that stretched to every horizon. Sometimes they were tall, sometimes they were short. Sometimes they were older, sometimes they were younger. They were all amazingly good looking. But no matter their circumstances, they shared the same single-minded goal, losing long nights of sleep over it, working out a strategy that would surely work this time.

They only wanted to come home to me.

A man's hand rested on my shoulder. It jerked me out of my imaginary worlds and back into the gray room with the fluorescent lights. "It's okay, Bailey."

Ryan.

I flinched. He removed his hand as if he'd touched something hot. He was trying so freaking hard to get through to me. Had been since the day he'd met me, barely a week ago. But it was too late. I didn't trust anyone anymore, unless they existed in my imagination. No one could hurt me in there, unless I let it happen as part of the story. No one could abandon me there, unless I planned a dramatic, tear-jerking reunion afterwards. If life had taught me anything, it was that such happy endings were not for the real world. My heart was sitting, alone and dying, in the bottom of the deep freezer.

"I don't see anything," I lied. "I can't remember what he looked like." The murderer. I finally opened my eyes and looked at the detective, Monica Steele. Her eyes were icy and barricaded. They were like mine. Her heart was in a deep freezer, too. I wondered who had put it there. "I'm sorry. I can't remember."

She met my gaze, her eyes like steel—maybe that's where she got her name. She wanted me to say what the killer looked like. But I didn't know. Everything had happened too fast. I'd been busy trying not to die. And now all I wanted to do was die. If only I'd known that then.

The tension in our eyes was perfectly matched, the detective and me, like people arm wrestling. I knew I would win. I had my whole, pathetic, meaningless life in front of me to do nothing but sit and stare. She had deadlines.

Suddenly her hardened eyes softened. The change was almost imperceptible. It was not like a dam breaking. It was like a single drop of water squeezing through a crack, running down the wall. She turned away before I could see any more, before I could get past the barricade in her eyes. What did it mean, that tiny crack?

Empathy. She saw herself in me—a soul that had been let down far too many times, or crushed so badly there was no putting it back together. She hadn't felt empathy for another living soul for years. Not since her heart had been broken.

Maybe I was just making all that up. I can't read minds. But survival had taught me how to read faces, so I'll stand by what I said. She saw herself in me.

"Thanks for trying, Bailey," she said. She wasn't pretending to be kind anymore. She meant it this time. Her military-like posture had loosened, though she didn't look at me. She shuffled her papers and pen. "If you remember anything about him, let me know."

I nodded.

Ryan eyed me carefully, as if I might explode. He didn't try to touch me again. "Shall I take you home?"

I wished he'd give up on me. But I knew he'd have a fit if I tried to walk home in the dark. I nodded.

For a moment, I tried to picture Ryan as one of the many reincarnations of my father. I scrapped that prototype immediately—which was weird, when I thought about it. Not only was he flesh-and-blood; he lived the life of danger and heroism that I constantly pictured my dad in.

Something about the realness of Ryan Brandt scared me. Make-believe would never be more than a dream and a Band-Aid. But my dreams always ended happily. Real life never did.

He stood, his gear and body armor protesting.

I didn't move. Not yet. There was something I wanted to know. It was my turn to ask the questions, though somehow I couldn't get my voice above a whisper. "What did you do with the necklace?" I asked. The silver ship's wheel on the tarnished ball chain.

Ryan lowered a brow at me. "Why did he give that to you?"

I kicked the leg of my chair and shrugged. "I have no idea." I really didn't. The man with the wavy hair had pressed it into my palm just before he died. He'd been really adamant I keep it. I'd promised I would. But why did I even care?

I guess because the dead man had cared.

"It's being kept as evidence," Ryan said. "We'll get it back to you when we can."

Which in my experience meant never. It didn't matter. Nothing mattered.

When I didn't move, Ryan held out his hand, inviting. "C'mon, Bailey. Let's get you home."

Home. Peachy. I scooted off my chair and followed Ryan to his patrol car. To my "home."

To Bud.

8

CHAPTER TWO
MONICA

I flicked off the video and audio recorders then gathered up my notes as Ryan opened the door for Bailey. He guided her ahead of him like a breeze blowing a leaf across a pond. With their backs turned, I allowed myself to slump and catch my breath. Something had happened just now—between me and Bailey—and I was still recovering. Trying to make sense of how it could have happened.

The Wall had come down. The personal defense system I'd been putting together, one component at a time, for the past ten years. In a single moment, security had been completely breached. Emergency sirens wailed inside my head and lights flashed. It was chaos.

Ryan glanced back over his shoulder. His brow wavered. Crap. I'd let him see me looking vulnerable. I pulled my shoulders back and stuffed papers into my portfolio.

"I'll be right there," Ryan said to the girl. When she was out of sight, he turned to me and whispered, "You okay?"

"Fine," I said. "Exhausted." Between the rumbling aftershocks of the Wall's downfall and all the shit that had been going down lately, I simply didn't have the energy to be snarky to Ryan. I glanced up at him and lifted an eyebrow. "You?"

He nodded. "Tired."

"Black and blue I suppose?"

He rubbed his chest. "Sore," he admitted.

An officer-involved shooting—Ryan's—was just one of the many shits gone down. Thank God he'd been wearing his body armor.

Then again, why was I so relieved? I'd spent the past ten years calling down curses on his head. Any man who cheated on me deserved my eternal wrath—especially a man who'd wedded and bedded me, only to chase the first pretty ass that swung by. Ryan and I simply hadn't been meant to last, I suppose. He was a dick. I was a bitch.

I zipped shut my portfolio and sat on the edge of the table. "We *must* be tired. Look at us, actually holding a civil conversation."

He grinned but didn't reply. Smart man. He knew that any words with me could end in fireworks; I was just that volatile. Hence the Wall. It existed as much to keep myself locked in as to keep other people locked out.

He cocked his head toward the lobby. "I'd better get Bailey home." Clearly making an exit while his luck lasted.

I dropped my gaze into my lap and nodded.

He left. The door clicked shut behind him. I remained sitting. I should have tried to get him to stay longer. Just another minute or two while the Wall was down. This kind of opportunity wasn't likely to happen again in either of our lifetimes.

I'd laid the cornerstone back when Ryan Brandt had cheated on me. I'd never meant to embark on such a large-scale building project. I'd never even noticed the pieces moving into place, brick by brick. But when I'd eventually noticed it, I embraced it. It was *my* Wall. I found it was good against all sorts of things. Lying suspects, violent detainees, hardened criminals of every sort. It was even good against heartbreak: children who died in car accidents, entire families who perished in house fires, wives battered at the hands of their own husbands.

People were intimidated by the Wall. They sensed it the moment I walked into a room, and spines visibly straightened. The Wall was both my protection and my power; my armor and my weapon. No one had ever broken down the Wall.

Until tonight.

In the end, it hadn't succumbed to cannonade or machine gun fire or military-grade explosives. It had been broken by a child.

Which was fitting in a way.

She wasn't afraid to look me in the eye. She'd marched straight through the laser network. She had a Wall, too, and hers was better than mine. That's what had caused the breach in the first place: the shock. No girl so young should have a Wall so tough. I could harden myself against anything—except a clone of myself that hadn't even graduated high school yet.

What could have broken her so badly to erect that iron barricade? And was there any hope for her?

I sighed and finished packing my portfolio. I hit the lights on my way out of the interview room and found Chief Wade Erickson in the hall, moving toward the elevator.

"Chief. Any luck?"

He stopped and shook his head. "No sign of the get-away car." His tall frame hung loosely and his eyes were dull. He was exhausted, too.

"Someone will spot it."

He glanced at me quizzically. I only realized then that it was probably the first time in ten years that I'd played the optimist. I simply backed it up with a smile as if it were par for the course.

"What about leads?" I asked. "Could Roland give us any names?"

He pulled a worn notebook from his shirt pocket and sighed, hoisting his eyebrows. "Yes," he said, eying his own scrawl. "At first blush, I doubt any of them are a match. Most of these people are in their seventies and eighties."

I ran a hand down the side of my face. "I'll go through the list in the morning."

"Neumiller will. I want you to take a three-day weekend. You've been going non-stop."

I lifted my portfolio. "I've got so much—"

Wade put his hand on it and pushed it back down. "Lehman and Neumiller will both be here tomorrow. You'll spell Neumiller on Tuesday and Lehman on Wednesday. You've pulled your weight. Go home. Recharge your batteries."

I ground my teeth. I could rebuild the Wall faster at work. At home I'd have nothing to do but stare in shocked dismay at the wreckage. But with all my offensive strategies in disarray, there was no fighting the chief this time.

"Yes, Sir," I muttered.

"Good. I'll see you Tuesday." He turned and began to walk away.

"Chief?"

He paused and looked back. "Yes?"

My mouth went dry on the words I had to ask. "Did you tell Tommy?" The Mailboat captain. It was his son we'd found Bailey crying over in the street.

Wade chewed his lip and stared at the ceiling, sighing through his nose. "I'll tell him in the morning."

I scowled and glanced at my watch. "My God, Wade, someone should have told him hours ago."

"Let an old man get his sleep. It's not like he has anyone else to pass the news along to."

My jaw dropped. "Wade!"

He held up a hand and turned his gray eyes on me. For the first time since I'd known him, he looked old. Tired. "Monica, the rules don't always apply."

12

I closed my mouth, but refused to agree.

"I'll see you Tuesday." He turned down the hall and walked away.

I growled to myself and headed for my car. All too often, that man simply infuriated me. The instant I walked out into the night air, the reality of a three-day weekend hit me between the eyes. It would just be me and the Wall and that damn breach. The smoke and debris had cleared enough for me to get my first good look at the gash. It was vast. Emotions were pouring through like water spilling over a dam.

Never mind homicide. I had a bigger problem on my hands.

CHAPTER THREE
RYAN

The streets, normally glutted with tourists in daylight, were dead quiet after midnight. I took my time on the drive to Bailey's house. By habit, my eyes scanned for anomalies—shadows moving inside the dimly-lit gift shops and boutiques, doors ajar on the quaint cottages and Victorian homes. But it was finally quiet in Lake Geneva. The radio in the cruiser was silent. Even the pink and white petunias hanging from the lamp posts were folded up, their heads bowed as they slumbered.

I glanced now and again at my passenger, Bailey Johnson, and kept the patrol car moving just below the speed limit, trying to buy time, hoping to come up with something to say that would finally make an inroad in the barrier between Bailey and the world.

Working law enforcement my whole career, I'd seen my fair share of human hardship and the resulting broken spirits. Most days, I didn't let it get to me. But something about Bailey got under my skin and wouldn't leave. She was so alone. She had literally no one in her corner shouting her on. And I couldn't erase from my memory the fact that it had been my hands that handed her over to the foster care system eleven years ago. I had blithely moved on to new departments, new adventures, a thousand new lives.

And Bailey was still here. Alone. I shouldn't feel responsible for her. But I did.

She directed her gaze out her open window, the breeze playing with the strands of hair that always slipped loose from her ponytail. Even from this angle, I could make out her fading black eye.

I'd tried to get her to tell me who had given her that mark, but she was sealed like a tomb. Her foster dad, Bud Weber, wasn't admitting to anything, either, and her nearly non-existent social circle could provide no leads.

I finally ventured to speak. "So, what happened to your arms?"

She scrunched her nose and shook her head as if the question were stupid and meaningless. "Nothing," she said.

"Doesn't look like nothing." I stole a glance for the dozenth time. Purple and blue smudges marred her outer forearms. By their positioning, they looked like self-defense wounds.

"I'm a klutz," she said. "I walk into everything."

"You seem to manage mail jumping okay." They didn't hire klutzes at the Mailboat. You had to get off and on the boat at top speed to get the mail in the boxes.

She said nothing. Only filled her lungs and sighed. The slant of her eyebrow, the one I could see, was angry. Captain Tommy Thomlin had tipped us off to her bruises. I half expected he was the one she was angry with.

The question was why she resented me, and perhaps Tommy, for asking. Why she still refused to name her abuser. I knew in my gut that our culprit was her foster dad. I'd met the man and wasn't impressed. But as much as I trust my instincts on the street, they don't help a lot in a court of law. I didn't have any evidence. Nothing that could justify twirling my handcuffs around my finger and coolly slipping them over Weber's wrists while I uttered the

Miranda warning. Instead, I sat idly by as Bailey harvested new injuries. It heated my blood just to think about it.

"You doing all right, Bailey? You got through quite a shit show tonight." Ever since we'd found her in the middle of the street after tonight's gun battle, the only one standing—the only one *alive*—she had been shockingly stoic. Emotionless. A few tears. That was all.

She didn't answer and simply wrapped a strand of hair around her finger. I'd never known another human being who could maintain a stony silence as long as she could. I was pretty sure I could drive three times around the world, and still be waiting for a reply. She was lost in her own head. Lost in a world that only got worse, never better. My heart cracked every time I looked at her.

"Do you have anyone you can talk to?"

Silence.

It didn't matter. I already knew the answer. She'd told me before that she didn't have any friends.

I quit trying to make conversation.

Minutes later, I pulled into her driveway, the cement cracked and crumbling into the street. The house wasn't much better. A contrast to the idyllic homes that dotted almost every neighborhood in town, this one was short a few shingles and looked out on the world through filthy windows. The paint was peeling off the sills.

I'd seen her foster dad's place of business, the Geneva Bar and Grill, and it was a veritable palace by comparison. Granted, it looked like a remodeled corrugated tin barn, strung with a confusing mix of neon bar signs and pirate paraphernalia. But at least the amenities were clean, updated, and maintained. There was no question where Bud's loyalties lay. They weren't at home, and they weren't with Bailey, of that I was sure.

I shifted into park. Bailey unbuckled her seatbelt and popped open the door without a word to me.

"Bailey?"

16

She jumped out of the car as if she hadn't heard me.

I leaned across the console and the metal bracket holding my laptop. "Bailey!"

Her shoulders visibly drooped, but she halted. She tilted her head back, as if she were staring away at the stars. As if she wanted to be sucked into the cosmos.

"We have a police chaplain. He's a great guy. I'll set you up with him, if you like."

She said nothing.

I chewed my cheek. "I guess I'll take that for a yes." It was a fairly safe bet. From previous conversations, I'd concluded she didn't care what happened in her life one way or the other. She'd probably stopped caring a long time ago.

I stared at her back and wanted desperately to get out of the car and force her into a bear hug. I wanted to hug her until she cried. And then I wanted to hold her some more, until she'd wrung out every last tear that she'd been bottling up inside for God only knew how long. I shuddered to think how many tears she was hiding, merely because no one had ever been there to wipe them away.

I'd never felt this way about a child. A voice in the back of my head said this was what it felt like to have kids of your own. It scared the piss out of me. I'd always assumed I'd make the world's lousiest dad. Monica, as my ex-wife, no doubt agreed. If I couldn't remain faithful to a woman, how was I supposed to stick around long enough to raise kids? In the grand scheme of things, maybe it was a blessing we'd never had a family.

Bailey began to slide away, as if testing whether I'd stop her this time. I didn't. I was fresh out of excuses to make her stay. She swung the door shut and sprinted up the driveway to the house without a look back.

I drummed my thumbs on the steering wheel and released a sigh. I wouldn't rest until I'd proved the identity of whatever party or parties were responsible for her bruises; until that person was locked in a cell and Bailey was free to live the life of a normal sixteen-year-old. But beyond that, perhaps I should just give up. It was my job to ensure her safety, not her happiness. And she was making it abundantly clear she didn't want my interference in her life.

It didn't matter anyway. I was only a reserve officer, hired on to help with the busy tourist season in my hometown. When summer ended, I'd be moving on. I was a drifter—always had been—and in a few short months, I'd be drifting on again.

CHAPTER FOUR
BAILEY

I ran up the driveway and threw myself against the front door. But half-way over the threshold, I changed tack from flight to stealth. I landed on tip-toes. Held my breath. Searched the darkness inside. Truth be told, I was more afraid of what lay ahead of me than what lay behind. Much as I hated being scrutinized by Officer Brandt, at least he'd never whipped me with a belt.

The lights were out. The TV was dark. Those were good signs. Maybe Bud was asleep—passed out on the sofa or in his bed or in some weird place like under the sink. There was no telling where he might turn up when he was drunk. He usually was. I couldn't fathom how he got up early every morning to open the restaurant. As far as I could tell, he didn't care a whit about hangovers. Maybe he'd developed a resistance, like bugs do to pesticides.

My sins were now neck-deep. I'd slipped out of the restaurant last night before my shift ended. I'd borrowed Bud's car. I'd gotten it stolen by an escaped murderer. But only after I'd gotten it shot through with bullets. In my defense, I was trying to stop a kidnapping. But after everything I'd done, I may as well hand Bud a cat-of-nine-tails and tie myself to a whipping post. I doubted he'd be overly comforted that I'd survived the street shooting. He'd simply be mad about the car. And he'd make sure I didn't walk away without some souvenir of the night's adventures.

Ryan and Tommy probably assumed I was scared what Bud would do to me if I said anything. I let them think so. But Bud wasn't my first fear.

Moving was.

If Ryan took Bud out of the picture, social services would have to find me a new placement. Again. I could end up anywhere in Walworth County. I could even be farmed out to another county. It may as well have been anywhere in the world.

I didn't want to move. Not now. Not when my life was as close to perfect as it had ever come. Maybe that sounded stupid. But it was true. All thanks to one person. One person who had turned my world upside-down.

But maybe that perfect world was all just a dream and it would only melt as soon as I reached out to touch it, like all dreams do. But dreams were all I had to live on.

I closed the door behind me silently, a millimeter at a time, and latched it without a click. Slowly I scanned the living room, lit only by the street lamp outside. The coffee table was littered with empty beer cans, a half-eaten bag of chips, and a flurry of magazines, mostly featuring shirtless men with giant dumbbells. As if Bud cared about fitness. Maybe he only had dreams to live on, too.

As my eyes soaked in the darkness, they suddenly made out a long, bulky form stretched across the sofa. I nearly gasped out loud but clapped a hand over my mouth just in time. I stood stock still and watched the shadow. It didn't move. Didn't breathe. Didn't stir. Slowly the mass took on more shape. The folds of a blanket. The fringed and frayed edge of a throw pillow. But the blanket was empty. Merely a crumpled shell, not even big enough to account for all of Bud.

I stood and breathed for a few minutes, simply waiting for my heart to slow down. Finally I peeled my hand from my mouth and tip-toed through the living room. In the hall, I played a sort of hopscotch, avoiding all the places where the floor creaked. I'd been living here for two years now, so I knew where the noisy spots were and could sneak in and out of my room whenever I needed. By this point in my life, I'd been in so many different foster placements, I could learn a new squeaky floor pattern within two days. Sometimes I felt that in Bud's house it didn't matter. It was like he had a sixth sense for my presence.

Or absence.

He had to know I'd left the restaurant early.

And he had to be furious.

But what else was I supposed to do? I'd seen a man kidnapped in our own parking lot, and I couldn't find Bud to tell him what was happening. I suppose a normal person would have called the police. But ever since the night they'd arrested my mother and sent me to my first foster home, I'd sort of gone out of my way to avoid them.

I was really failing at that lately. It seemed Officer Brandt popped up every time I turned around.

Okay, I could admit it now: Life with my mom and her boyfriends had been pathetic. What five-year-old is supposed to figure out how to feed herself? I still remembered putting the can of soup in the microwave, can and all. It was pretty epic, actually. Sparks flying everywhere... The aftermath wasn't nearly so cool. I still remembered the bruises from my mother's boyfriend-of-the-day. I think he was high. My mom and her boyfriends were always high.

But life in foster care hadn't been much of an improvement. The good placements never lasted, and the bad ones dragged on forever.

Like this one. I was pretty sure I was going to be stuck here until I aged out of the system. Only two years to go. Yippee. And then what? It was sink or swim, and knowing the general course of my life, I put my money on sink. Since the day I was born, I'd never managed more than an occasional gasp of air before going under again.

I held my breath now as I neared Bud's room. My door was just across the hall from his. The squeakiest floorboards were right between the two, a veritable pool of death. It was always a stretch to make it over the danger zone and through my own door without a sound. I peered into Bud's room first.

The blankets were rumpled but empty. It was dark except for red digital numbers shining out from a bedside clock. He wasn't there.

I leapt over the squeaky trap into my room and shut the door quickly but silently. Without bothering to change into pajamas—the tee shirt and sweat pants the cops gave me were essentially pajamas anyway—I simply kicked my shoes off and dove under the blankets. I pulled the covers tight over my head and curled into a ball.

I finally let myself cry. Tears only, no sobbing. Just in case Bud really was here somewhere or came home. I didn't need to attract his attention.

My brain was exploding. I tried to slip into another pretend story, someplace I could comfort myself and start to make sense of everything and end things the way I wanted them to. But I couldn't get a storyline started. My mind didn't know where to begin. So I just cried... and cried... and cried...

Until my thoughts ran away to the Mailboat.

The instant I pictured the navy-and-white tour boat, my mind slowed and calmed. I imagined the deck rocking beneath my feet as the nose broke through the waves. I climbed out onto the rub rail, my hand full of envelopes. Tommy piloted us toward the next pier. When the boat passed within three feet, I jumped over the open water and stuffed the mail into the box on the pier. Then I spun and ran back, leaping gracefully, and landed once again on the rub rail.

It was a dance. A ballet. Neither the boat nor I ever stopped. We had too many deliveries to make. So I ran. And she slipped through the water like a swan.

No, more like a whale. No boat that big should ever have been expected to perform maneuvers as precise as the Mailboat did. I couldn't do my job without Tommy behind the helm. Come wind or high water, he navigated the Mailboat within three or four feet of each pier, as precisely as a Swiss watch. He could easily have knocked over a dock, or crashed into a moored boat, or plowed down a poorly-placed inflatable swim toy.

But he never did.

He'd been driving the Mailboat for just about forever. It was an extension of his own body. It was like the wind and the waves were in his soul. They never surprised him, no matter what they did.

I felt safe in his hands.

It dawned on me I wasn't crying anymore. The Mailboat always seemed to have that effect on me. There was nothing but sunshine and sparkling water, white piers and smiles. I sighed and closed my eyes and hugged the fleeting sense of peace close to my chest.

I was scheduled to be at the Mailboat in the morning. A sane person would probably have asked for the day off. Not me. I needed to see the Mailboat again. I needed to see Tommy. Everything would be better when I got there. I would finally be okay.

More than anyone—more than kick-ass heroes from movies and novels, more than random, cool-looking people I met day-to-day and roped into my imaginary worlds— more than anyone, I daydreamed about Tommy. *He* was the dream I didn't dare to touch. The world I wanted but wouldn't ask for, knowing it would only melt away. With him, I never imagined big, heroic stuff, like shooting down enemies or blowing up extermination camps.

I simply pretended that he loved me.

CHAPTER FIVE
TOMMY

I was up early the next morning, packing my old canvas rucksack—drab tan with the words "US NAVY" patched on the front. Collectors would call it a rare item, an antique from the years between Korea and Vietnam. Back in its day, it had merely been standard issue. My uniforms then had borne no higher insignia than a petty officer second class. Now it carried my captain's uniform—but seeing as I was only the captain of a tour boat, it was hard to say who outranked who. I would have voted for the petty officer.

I folded my work clothes carefully to avoid wrinkles and preserve the pleats: a crease along the white shirt sleeves, a sharp fold down the front of the khaki shorts. Then they went into the bag to change into later. No sense getting them dirty while I cleaned and serviced the Mailboat before the tour.

My eye wandered to the picture on my bedside table. Elaina smiled up at me from our wedding day, as vivid to me now as if it had been yesterday. She wore a simple white dress with a little jacket and a pill box hat obscured in a cloud of netting. Her bobbed black hair just brushed her chin, while she looked up at me with doe eyes and a smile that could still move me to swim oceans, if it would have pleased her. She had been a beauty.

The necklace resting between her collarbones was the plainest piece of jewelry a bride had ever worn: a silver ship's helm on a ball chain like the one that had carried my dog tag. But she wouldn't have traded it for all the gold in the world. She had given me that charm the day I graduated high school and joined the Navy. She'd made me promise to bring it back to her some day.

And I did. As often as I could, until I got the petty officer's rate and pay grade. Then I came home, marched straight to the diner where Elaina worked, dropped to one knee, and presented her with both the helm and a diamond ring.

She didn't say yes. She simply kissed me on the mouth, in front of God and the world and a room full of breakfast eaters. I took it to mean she could stomach the idea of being stuck with me forever.

The ring I still had. I wondered where the charm was. Our son was the last to have it. Yet I didn't remember seeing it on him last night. Then again, I'd been too busy telling him how much he disgusted me.

I reached for my watch and twisted the wind-up mechanism, adding tension to the springs. Why Jason had played the risk—showing his face—I couldn't fathom. A fugitive for seventeen years, he still had a string of high-end burglaries to pay for. And a murder.

I'd let him walk away. But only after I was sure he knew I despised him.

Maybe I should have let him talk.

The day Jason left for college, Laina had given him a kiss in the kitchen, surrounded by his suitcases, and fastened the helm around his neck. "It will always bring you home," she said. Little did we know, he had already come unmoored from everything we'd ever taught him.

Granted, I never saw him without that charm. But where was it now? He'd probably thrown it away long ago, along with the rest of his life. His mother's. Mine.

Bailey's.

Bailey. I dropped heavily to the edge of the bed. Grasped the wristwatch in my fist. Pressed my fist to my mouth. Last night's revelation seared through my memory, tilting my entire existence on its head.

Jason had fathered a child. Not just any child. Bailey. I'd known my own granddaughter for over a year, without even knowing it. She was my mail girl.

Was there any such thing as coincidence? Truth be told, I'd felt drawn to her from her first day on the Mailboat. I'd thought it was because her upside-down, inside-out, cock-eyed way of looking at the world made me laugh like I hadn't in years. Or because she was an angel who had tripped over her own shoelaces and mussed her feathers while trying to find her way back to heaven. But maybe it had been more than that. Perhaps my DNA had recognized their own copies, as if stumbling across a mirror where you least expected to find one.

Some brute was laying hands on her and sending her off to me every morning with welts and bruises. There was no question about stepping in for Bailey. Ending the abuse. Making sure she was safe. That much I could do, and I would.

But then what? Was I ready to be her grandfather? My stomach roiled and the pressure that had been building in my head since last night peaked. I ground my fist against my temple.

At best, I could offer Bailey a grandfather who had failed as a father. At worst, I could let her know that her own dad was a thief, a killer, and a fugitive. What good would either one of us be to her?

I sat up straight and clapped the watch over my wrist, then slung the strap of the rucksack over my shoulder and grabbed my keys. I wouldn't say anything yet. I'd give myself time to think.

The doorbell chimed through the empty house. I glanced at the light slanting through my bedroom window. The sun was barely over the horizon. Who would be up this early?

I descended the stairs to the living room and glanced through the bow window. Wade stood on the porch. In uniform. It was Saturday. Why was he working on a Saturday?

Jason.

The thought punched me in the gut. They'd finally found him. Or was there a chance my son had done as I'd told him, and turned himself in? I doubted it. More likely than not, he'd tripped in his own tangled webs and fallen into the waiting arms of the law. Heart thumping, I threw back the lock and opened the door.

"Tommy."

"Wade. What is it? I was just leaving for work."

Wade chewed his lip. "I think you'd better call in."

"Why?" Wade's eyes were veiled. Sad. Bailey sprang to mind and my imagination shot to the worst conclusions. Her foster dad had attacked her again. Landed her in the hospital this time. Broken her bones. "Is this about Bailey?" I asked.

Wade shook his head.

Relief flooded me. "Then what is it?"

Wade worked his jaw before making his one-word reply. "Jason."

My heart skipped a beat. It was true, then. He was in custody.

I shut my eyes momentarily. Gripped the brass doorknob in one hand and the wooden frame in the other. I let the cold, hard reality sink in. That void—that endless void of waiting for answers I never wanted to hear—was over. Jason had been caught. The smug self-righteousness

28

I'd craved was oddly missing right when I'd expected to find it. Now that it came down to it, I didn't want justice for my son.

I simply wanted my son.

I opened my eyes to face the new reality. This new world I'd thought I'd wanted for so long. "You arrested him?" I asked.

Wade shook his head.

What did he mean? For a fleeting moment, I entertained the fantasy that it had all been some unfathomable mistake. That Jason was innocent. Of everything. I envisioned a table set with mounds of humble pie, and me savoring every bite.

"He's dead, Tommy."

I stared.

A dog barked somewhere and my neighbor's sprinkler system sputtered to life.

Dead?

No, that was impossible. I'd spoken with Jason just last night. Hours ago. He was fine.

"Do you want me to call Robb?" Wade asked.

Call Robb. As in, call to say I wasn't coming to work? That's what people do when a family member dies; they call in. He really meant it, then. Jason was...

My brain finally found the route to my tongue. "How can he be dead?"

"Come here, Tommy." Wade motioned me toward the Adirondack chairs on my front porch. I let the rucksack slip to the floorboards and sat. Wade folded his tall form into the seat next to me. He looked me in the eye.

"Tommy, I so hate to tell you this. He was killed."

Killed.

I stared across the street. One of the sprinkler heads was broken, aimlessly sputtering a half-hearted stream while the rest arched gracefully over the lush lawn. The dog kept running up and down the picket fence in the neighboring yard. Some kind of terrier. It was always barking.

A minute dragged by. Two. I couldn't find words. Only feel a growing emptiness that gnawed on every tender part of my soul.

"How?" I finally asked.

"We're still working out the details," Wade said. "But it looks as if he was kidnapped and..." He stopped and worked his jaw again. "He died of gunshot wounds," he finished.

Gunshot wounds. I'd seen him just last night. I'd spoken to him. I'd unleashed all my pent-up fury on him and sent him away. My last act as his father. I'd sent him away to his death.

I buried my face in my hands. "Dear God."

"I'll call Robb," Wade said quietly.

I shook my head. "No."

"Tommy, you're not driving the Mailboat today."

I nearly snapped at him that I most certainly *was*. What had I done the day Jason killed a cop and skipped town? I'd driven the Mailboat. What had I done the day my wife died? I'd driven the Mailboat. Today of all days, I craved normalcy. Routine. I wanted everything to be as it always was. I wanted my son.

That's all I'd ever wanted.

I just wanted my son.

"You know I'd never ask you this unless I had to," Wade said. "But I need you to come with me this morning. I need you to give me a positive identification."

My eyes snapped to his. It wasn't positive?

At the look of hope on my face, Wade's expression saddened. "For protocol, Tommy."

I stared at my friend, wishing there was some way to turn back the clock. Some way to return to those idyllic days when I had both Elaina and Jason and everything had been happy. Now here I was, alive but alone, and feeling as dead as I could possibly be.

The silver helm was gone. It had failed us in the end.

"Tell me this isn't happening, Wade," I whispered hoarsely.

He shook his head. "I wish I could."

CHAPTER SIX
BAILEY

The next morning, I walked over the brick walkway and past the angel fountain toward the Mailboat pier, backpack slung over my shoulder, as if nothing had happened the night before. I wanted to come to the Mailboat and have everything be normal. Whatever normal was. I guess I'd never done normal.

I stared at the bricks and read the same donor memorials etched in the stone as I'd read every day. I just wanted to see Tommy. My anchor. The one person who never changed. I wanted him to be my sounding board, like he had been for so many other things—mostly dumb stuff like how I'd saved a mouse from certain death. When Tommy was around, I was used to spitting out whatever was in my head and having him listen or laugh or... mostly laugh, come to think of it. I guess most of what's in my head is pretty dumb.

But I wanted to know what he'd say this time, anyway. I was pretty sure he wouldn't laugh. I wanted him to give me a hug and tell me I'd done everything I could have and that everything was going to be okay.

But when I rounded the corner onto the pier, the doors on the Mailboat were still shut. I gave the handle a twist, but it didn't move. The boat was locked.

That was weird. I pulled my phone out of my pocket and checked the time. Ten minutes before the hour, on the dot. I'd discovered, through experimentation, that Tommy always showed up ten minutes ahead of schedule. Therefore, so did I. Sometimes fifteen. I glanced up and down the pier, but I was the only one there, like a goose that had flown north for the winter.

I didn't have a key. I let my backpack slide to the pier, stepped onto the rub board, and sat on the bow of the boat, swinging my legs over the water. Tommy would be here soon.

Five minutes dragged by. Then six. Then seven.

I began to worry—and not just about Tommy being late. I wasn't going to have a chance to tell him what had happened. Michaela, the other jumper today, would be here soon. I didn't want to talk in front of her. But my stomach churned at the thought of keeping everything stuffed down inside for a whole extra day.

The top of the hour came and went, and I was still the only one here.

Had someone rescheduled Daylight Savings and forgotten to tell me? I checked my phone a hundred times. Even Googled *current time in lake geneva wi.*

It really was ten minutes *after* seven. Google knows everything.

Should I call Robb? This was really weird. Tommy ran everything by the clock. They set Big Ben by his comings and goings at the Mailboat.

I finally spied someone walking towards the piers in the familiar red polo shirt of the cruise line.

But it wasn't Tommy.

The slender, bald-headed man waved at me as he came near. "Morning, Bailey."

"Brian?"

"Sorry to keep you waiting." He pulled a ring of keys out of his pocket and pushed one into the lock on the door. "Robb only called me about twenty minutes ago. You've never seen a man down his eggs and bacon so fast as I did. I figured you'd get here before me, anyway."

Brian was one of several captains who drove the eight boats of the cruise line fleet, though he jokingly referred to himself as the "expendable crewman." He didn't have a regular boat or a regular tour anymore. Theoretically, he was retired. But he filled in whenever another captain couldn't be there or asked for time off.

Tommy had asked for time off?

"Where's Tommy?" I asked.

"Couldn't make it this morning," Brian replied.

"Is he sick?"

"I don't know what's up. Robb didn't say. Just told me Tommy might need the next few days off. Must be pretty important for him to let anybody else touch his boat." Brian laughed.

"Yeah, I guess." Tommy was pretty particular about "his" Mailboat.

"Boy, it's been years since I drove a Mailboat tour," Brian chattered on, fastening the doors in their open position. "Not since I had hair. The piers on the lake are all shaking in their boots. Won't be surprised if a few of them are sacrificed to the cause this morning."

I tried to laugh at his banter, but couldn't. This was the first day in the history of the Mailboat that Tommy was missing a tour. Well, maybe not the first ever, since Brian had apparently driven the tour before. But this was the first while I'd been a mail girl.

I hated it.

It blew my mind to think Tommy had been here every day for nearly fifty years. Constancy like that didn't exist in my world. One day, you could start to believe maybe your foster family was really going to be there for you. Maybe they were even going to adopt you or something. And then they'd move or have a baby of their own or just decide to quit foster care, and all of a sudden it was "moving day" again.

But Tommy had been on the Mailboat every day for, like, forty-eight years or something.

Until this morning.

Last week, he had been all concerned about me, asking questions, trying to figure out where my bruises were coming from. And now—when I really needed him—he didn't even show up.

I should have known better than to believe in people.

CHAPTER SEVEN
TOMMY

I stared at the photo.

I'd seen him less than twelve hours earlier. He'd had ruddy skin, warmed in the heat of argument. He'd been active. He'd been adamant.

He'd been alive.

The face in the photo was pale. Not even a black-and-white rendering could hide that. The eyes were closed, but not in repose. They were shutters, nailed down against a raging storm.

Wade leaned forward in his office chair and lifted a tentative eyebrow. "Tommy?"

I closed my eyes. He was waiting for an answer. I couldn't loosen my vocal chords enough to speak. So I nodded.

Wade slipped the print-out from between my fingers. "Okay. I'm sorry. I needed your opinion. He's changed some since…"

Since his face had first been flashed on the six o'clock news. *If you have any information regarding the whereabouts of Jason Thomlin…* a serious but dispassionate voice echoed through my mind.

"I know," I said. You could also say he'd changed some since last night. But I didn't mention it. The fact that I'd spoken with Jason last night complicated things. A lot of things...

Wade pushed the sheet of paper into a cubbyhole out of sight. He'd spared me the trip to the morgue in Elkhorn and pulled up the photo from a database on his computer, correctly assuming that I'd be more comfortable in his office.

I hadn't told him yet that I'd seen Jason. Should I? No doubt Wade was up to his eyes right now, triangulating Jason's every move. Perhaps he'd figure it out himself.

Come to think of it, we'd both be better off if he didn't.

I couldn't tell Wade that I'd let my son go—a wanted man, a killer. It wouldn't do any good now to explain that I'd told Jason to turn himself in. He obviously hadn't. That made things muddy. Strictly speaking, I'd aided and abetted a criminal. Would Wade raise charges against me if he knew the truth? No. He'd be frustrated with me, but he wouldn't do anything about it. I didn't need to tarnish his badge by letting him cover for me.

But this meant I could never be fully honest with my best friend about the last time I'd seen my only son. By extension, I couldn't tell Wade what I'd learned from that last conversation. That Bailey was my granddaughter.

How long could I keep a secret like that locked away?

"Wade, who did this?"

He twisted his office chair back and forth, avoiding my eyes and rubbing his upper lip. "We're still working on it," he said through his hand.

Meaning he knew, but wouldn't say. It was an ongoing investigation. There were some rules he wouldn't bend. Even for me. My jaw tightened. "Wade, this is my *son*."

He merely shook his head without looking at me. My anger boiled. I opened my mouth, but he headed me off.

"I'll tell you when I have all the facts. For now, suffice it to say the party responsible paid their dues. Jason didn't go down without a fight."

"Then the killer's dead?" There was some comfort in that.

"One of them. We're still trying to identify the accomplice and track him down."

The fleeting sense of assurance vanished. "Do you have any leads?"

"Our witness wasn't able to provide a description. But we have fingerprints, ballistics… Hopefully we'll learn something."

"Is this connected to Fritz's death?" I asked. Less than a week ago, one of my son's old cronies had been murdered, too. Bailey had found the body at the end of a pier when she missed her jump back to the Mailboat and landed in the lake.

"Probably." Wade sat back, elbows on the armrests, and folded his hands across his stomach. "How are you doing, Tommy?" he asked.

It hurt. It hurt more than I could say. I'd told myself I didn't care about Jason anymore. I'd disowned him, after all. But dwelling on life's cruelties had never been my way. I stared into space several moments then shook my head. "My son died seventeen years ago."

Wade tilted an eyebrow, clearly unsatisfied with my answer. "Didn't you ever hope he might come back?"

"Why?" I asked. "He would have gone to prison. I would have gone on with my life." I rubbed my hands on my shorts, as if to clean them of the conversation. "It's better this way."

Wade's eyes dropped to my hands and flickered back up. "You know I don't buy that." He shrugged. "But whatever you say."

I remembered too late that I rubbed my palms when I was agitated. Wade no doubt knew that. Few things escaped his notice.

I stood up. "Do you need anything else?"

"Do *you?*"

I shrugged. "Just to go to work."

Wade shook his head, scowling. "Take the day off, dammit. You're already late."

I directed my conversation to the corner of the room again. "Brian will be filling in for me. He won't mind going home. He's supposed to be retired."

Wade cocked half a grin. "And you're not?"

I tried to dish up a clever comeback, but couldn't find the energy for humor. Instead, my thoughts took a heavier turn. No, I was not going to retire. I would have too much time on my hands. Too much time to think. And none of my thoughts were good these days.

When I didn't answer, Wade spoke again. "You're coming to my house tonight to have supper with Nancy and me." He punctuated his words by staring at me threateningly over the rims of his glasses. He lifted his eyebrows, as if daring me to refuse. "Cameron will be home. And Lindsey's coming over with the kids. You shouldn't be alone on a day like this."

"I'll think about it," I said. Which meant no, and Wade knew it. He lifted one eyebrow even higher. I spread my palms. "I'm fine, Wade. Really."

"I'll call you later."

"If it makes you feel better."

"It does."

I nodded. "Fine. I'll talk to you later, then."

Wade nodded, still staring at me like he wanted to pin me to the ground and torture me until I confessed my sorrows.

I turned to walk out.

"One more thing, Tommy."

I halted in the doorway but didn't look back. What was it now? I let Wade see me sigh. *Just give me some peace.*

"I thought you'd want to know."

"Yes? Know what?"

"Bailey was there."

I turned, confused but listening. "Where?"

"She was our witness."

A spike of solid ice skewered my heart. Bailey? Realization dawned—realization that was mine alone. Wade couldn't have guessed it in a million years. No one could have.

She had seen her father die.

But did *she* know that? Why had she been there? Had Jason tracked her down? Talked to her? It couldn't be a coincidence. It was unfathomable. Or were the Thomlin genes that magnetic? A silver helm built into our bloodstream? Was our shared DNA beckoning each other? Looking for mirrors, where they shouldn't expect to find any?

My palms broke out in a cold sweat and my mouth went dry. Had Jason told her? Suddenly, all the possibilities I hoped most to avoid were unavoidable.

I licked dry lips again. "Did she… Did she know who he was?"

With luck, Wade would take me to mean, did she know Jason was my son? But if luck had weighed anchor on me, Wade would understand the full meaning: Did she know Jason was also her father? If Jason had told her, the fact would have come out during the hours of police interview. I had no doubt of it. Wade could have been playing me this whole time. He might know as much as I did.

But he shook his head, looking down and twisting his chair again. "No. We asked what she knew about him, and she only said he talked to her at the grill when he stopped in for a sandwich. So far as she knows, he was just a random customer."

My heart dropped with relief. The secret was still safe. Wade would have been all over me like wolves to a carcass if he'd learned that Bailey was my granddaughter.

"We didn't tell her, either," he went on, oblivious. "Small town. Word travels. Makes investigation muddy. No one needs to know yet that Jason Thomlin died last night."

True enough. "I appreciate that, Wade."

He nodded.

"I'm going to work," I said.

Wade massaged the bridge of his nose and sighed. "There's no help for fools. Dinner's at six."

"I have a date with a wooden boat."

"Whatever."

I turned and walked away, still catching my breath.

Miraculously, it was possible no one knew. Not Wade. Not even Bailey. I still had time to decide what to do. Whether I should tell her... or whether I should spare her the pain. The pain of knowing she came from broken pieces; from the wreckage of ships washed ashore by a hurricane.

CHAPTER EIGHT
BAILEY

Michaela stepped onto the boat, staring down at her phone.

"Oh my *God*, have you people seen the news this morning?" She dumped her pink, bling-encrusted bag on the floor and scrolled down her screen. "There was another homicide last night—a double murder."

Brian sat on the edge of the hatch to the engine compartment and wiped grease off his hands with a dirty rag. "You don't say?"

Yanking open the cupboard doors, I grabbed the paper towel and window cleaner without asking Michaela how we were dividing responsibilities today. The jumper who cleaned the windows was also the jumper who went to the post office to get the mail, and I was determined to get away from the pier and this conversation as soon as possible.

It wasn't a *double murder*, I wanted to snap. The man with the wavy hair had killed the bald guy in self-defense.

In *my* defense.

I almost *died* last night.

I swallowed back a tsunami of tears and desperately snatched at the first happy, distracting thought that sprang to mind. *Puppies and kitties, and kitties and puppies, and puppies and kitties, and kitties and puppies…*

But the image of furry animals only reminded me of Humphrey, my rescue mouse that Bud had squashed, and I came close to crying again.

Michaela looked up from her phone and eyed Brian. She snapped the wad of gum in her mouth. "Tommy's got the day off?"

"Sick or somethin'. Who died?"

"No IDs yet. Can you believe this?"

I did. Far better than she knew. I attacked the windows with gusto, determined to finish them in record time and get the hell out of there.

Weird. I never wanted to be away from the Mailboat. But it was different today. It was different without Tommy.

I wiped away a tear before anybody could see it fall. I finished the windows in a flash, leaving streaks everywhere, and took off for the post office without saying goodbye to Michaela or Brian. Everything was backwards and upside down. Everything was wrong today, and I couldn't stand it.

An hour later when I'd collected and sorted the mail at the post office, I threw it all into a wheeled bin marked USPS and carted it back to the pier. It was nine a.m., and the day's passengers were already lined up behind the rope, waiting to board. I bypassed them with my cart. Exclamations and pointing fingers followed me like a wave.

"There she is! There's the mail jumper!"

Today, the notoriety failed to boost my mood.

I parked my cart by the large window near the front of the boat, the one that doubled as the mail jumper's entry and exit during deliveries. Come to think of it, I'd never questioned why we were given a window instead of a door, despite the fact this boat had been completely designed for mail delivery. It was one of the many things in my life that simply defied explanation. As with everything else, I just rolled with it. My life wasn't meant to make sense.

I grabbed a box of mail from the cart, stepped onto the rub rail, and leaned through the window to set the crate on the floor.

Inside, Tommy unstacked chairs and put them out in rows.

All my neurons fired at once and I nearly toppled head-first into the boat. "Tommy!"

He glanced up, flashed a brief smile, and went back to sorting chairs.

I grabbed two bags of mail from the push cart and jumped into the boat through the window. I beamed at Tommy. Of course he would never miss a day. Ever, ever, ever. Why had I doubted him? For an instant I was so happy, I forgot about unloading last night's crap on him.

"You feeling better?" I asked.

He looked at me, his face blank, as if my question made no sense. Then he shook his head, like clearing cobwebs. "Yeah," he finally said, straightening out the chairs. "Just a headache."

It had to have been a doozy to keep Tommy away from the Mailboat. But honestly, he looked like crap. Not a hint of color in his face. His eyes dead-pan. His shoulders slack. I eyed him cautiously. Where was the smile? The hello he usually handed out left and right like free tickets to the Greatest Show on Earth? Gone. It was all gone. Boom. Obliterated. It was like he'd pulled inside himself into a hard, cramped shell. As if, for the first time in his life, he didn't have the energy to give anyone a grin and a good morning.

Something was really wrong.

He stopped and stared at me, frozen, his mouth parted and his brow heavy. He studied me from head to foot and back again slowly, never saying a word.

What? I looked down at myself to make sure my shirt wasn't on backwards or something. Far as I could tell, I'd dressed myself correctly. So what was I doing wrong? Why was he staring at me?

Tommy licked his lips. "Bailey..."

I waited.

He stirred, as if waking from a reverie. Nodded to the front counter. "Better get those newspapers rolled." He turned abruptly toward a stack of chairs at the back of the boat.

Okay, that was totally weird. And I guess today was not the day to ask him to hear out my own problems. My shoulders slumped. I was going to have to tough everything out on my own.

A little piece of me died.

CHAPTER NINE
TOMMY

I wrangled the chairs into rows, angry with myself. How hard is it? How hard was it to sit Bailey down and tell her?

But it *was* hard. It was excruciating. I would have to tell her that her father had been a murderer. A fugitive. That these were the reasons he'd abandoned her before she was even born.

I'd also have to tell her that it didn't matter anymore. That he was dead.

That it was her own father she'd watched die.

The fact of my son's death hit me again like a wave, and I nearly lost it right there on the boat. I stiffened my jaw and willed myself through the pain.

Telling Bailey would also mean facing the fact that her welfare—the remainder of her upbringing—was my responsibility. And that was just a responsibility I wasn't qualified to take on. I'd raised a criminal. What good was I to Bailey?

No. I realized now. This was a secret I was meant to carry to my grave. The truth could only bring her pain— even more pain than it brought to me.

CHAPTER TEN
BUD

Bud threw a scorched pan down on the counter in the dish room. "You call that clean?" he bellowed at the dishwasher, a scrawny boy with dark hair stuck flat to his head. "Clean that right this time, you hear me?"

"Yes, sir," the kid replied. He pushed his fat, square glasses further up his nose before plunging the pan into a sink full of brown suds and attacking it with a wire scrubby. Dirty water splashed the sleeves of his over-sized tee shirt, plastering them to his arms while the drooping ends flapped like a pair of flippers.

Bud puckered a scowl at him, then stepped back into his kitchen and took another swig from his whiskey bottle. It was half gone, and it wasn't even noon yet. Worse, he was working on the second bottle. That much alcohol would lay a lesser man on the floor, but not Bud. He was made of tougher stuff, and he didn't plan to stop drinking any time soon—though he might switch to beer. It was getting hard to read the orders.

His phone call last night to The Man buzzed in his ears, along with the whiskey. *"Find out if Bailey recognized you. We may have to deal with her."*

How was he supposed to find out, without admitting to her that he was the goddamn killer? Well, him and Charles Hart. But Hart was dead as a post now, leaving Bud to take the fall—the inconsiderate ass. Would threats be enough to keep Bailey from telling the police? She'd been getting awfully buddy-buddy with them lately. Just the other day, that cop son-of-a-bitch had come around asking questions about Bailey's black eye.

Bud gazed into the bottle of fire water and saw his life unraveling. Worst of all, he saw his foster girl being taken away from him. He couldn't stomach it. That kid belonged with him.

Rita slapped a green slip of paper down on the window. "Order," she called.

"Damn you, make it yourself!" Bud shot back. He carried his whiskey with him into his office and slammed the door.

CHAPTER ELEVEN
BAILEY

When we got back to the pier, Tommy stayed for the next tour, but I changed into the clothes I'd brought for waitressing and headed across town for my second job. For once in my life, I almost didn't mind leaving the Mailboat. We got the mail delivered. We gave the tour. But everything just felt weird, and I couldn't understand why.

I cracked open the back door to the Geneva Bar and Grill and peered into the kitchen. A five-gallon kettle spluttered on the stove and a light glared in one of the ovens, highlighting a pan full of dinner rolls. But the room was empty. Thank God. With any luck, Bud was in the bar with his usual buddies, downing glasses of beer. My hope was that he would be just tipsy enough to be happy, but not so far gone as to be livid when he saw me. I was doing my darndest to avoid him—to avoid explaining why I'd skipped out during my shift last night and gotten his car shot through and stolen. Why I hadn't come home until after midnight.

I slipped through the door, danced across the tiles to the storeroom, and pulled my time card out of its slot. When exactly should I pencil in that I'd clocked out last

49

night? The schedule and my actual hours didn't align so good.

The grid on my time card blurred as I stared at it. I was so tired, it was getting hard to think straight. I'd worked a long day yesterday, survived a street shooting, and stayed up half the night being grilled by police, only to roll out of bed early again to run up and down the piers around the lake, delivering mail. And now here I was, putting in a shift at the restaurant. It vaguely dawned on me that no one should be expected to live like this. I leaned forward until my forehead hit the wall and simply stared at the bumps in the paint.

"Hey, where'dja go last night?"

I jumped.

Jimmy Beacon stood at his sink, water dripping on the floor from his sleeves, eyes magnified by his bulging glasses, as if he'd just emerged from a prehistoric swamp.

"Um... I just... I didn't feel good."

"Rita was looking everywhere for you. She was ready to explode. She had to work all the tables herself."

"Yeah, um... it came up really fast." I turned my back and pressed my time card and pencil close to my nose, hoping he would drop the conversation.

He didn't. Out of the corner of my eye, I saw him fling water off his hands and come around a counter piled with dirty dishes. He wiped his palms down his shirt. "Hey, Bailey, I was wondering if—"

"I'm busy."

He couldn't have been more taken aback if I'd slapped him in the face with a fish. "You don't even know what I was going to ask."

Actually, I did. He asked three times a week. Do you want to go out for ice cream? Do you want to catch a movie? Do you want to take a walk in the park? And the zinger: Do you want to see my secret lab? Despite putting the words *no thanks* on automatic repeat, I couldn't sit down for a break and a glass of soda without him sidling up next to me and talking my ear off.

"Um... Seriously, I've been really busy lately," I said, dog-earing a corner of my time card. "I'm working two jobs this summer." And like... trying to stay alive.

"You wouldn't have to work two jobs. Bud would give you all the hours you need here, you know."

The mere thought inspired an impulse to drown Jimmy in his own sink. Leave the Mailboat? For *this* place? "Great," I said out loud, hoping Jimmy didn't see me roll my eyes. "I'll talk to him about that."

His lips spread into a fleshy grin. "You will?"

Oh, God.

"Bailey!"

Bud's voice hit me like a sonic boom. Jimmy scurried back to his sink and attacked his stack of dishes with gusto. I whirled, trembling. My foster dad filled the doorway to his office, his unshaved face stormy, his eyes glassy but furious. I didn't need to glance at the bottle in his hand to know he was drunk.

"Get in here."

His tone told me everything I was afraid to hear. He knew. About his car. About skipping out last night. I was busted ten thousand different ways.

I gingerly stepped toward him. He grabbed my arm, shoved me into the office, and slammed the door behind us. The bottle he thunked down on his desk, which was covered in a snowdrift of paperwork, a few empty beer cans, and a dirty mouse trap. The mouse trap made me think of Humphrey. I began to cry.

He throttled me by both my shoulders. "Where's my car?"

"I'm sorry," I whimpered.

"So it *was* you? You took it, didja? When did you get a driver's license? Huh? Huh? When did I give you permission to drive my car? Answer me, kid."

"I'm sorry," I said again. "I looked for you. I couldn't find you."

"Oh, and you were gonna *ask* to drive my car?"

"No, I was going to tell you somebody got kidnapped. Out in the parking lot. I followed them. That's why I took the car."

His eyes widened into an insane sort of frenzy and his fists tightened on my arms. I had to get the rest out fast, before he dismissed the whole thing as bullshit and started belting me.

"There was a shooting!" I squeaked. "Two guys kidnapped one of our customers, and they tried to kill him. I mean, they did—they killed him. But he killed one of them back. The other one got away in your car. I don't know where he took it. I'm sorry."

I was shocked how stupid the whole thing sounded as it tumbled out of my mouth. I'd lied to Bud once or twice to get out of a beating, but now that I was telling the truth, it sounded like the worst fantasy a three-year-old could have drummed up.

So I was pretty surprised when the fury melted off Bud's face, replaced by a satisfied smile. He let me go and dropped into his office chair, which groaned alarmingly under his weight. "Kidnappers, eh?" he asked. He grabbed the whiskey and drank straight from the bottle. "That's funny." He laughed. "So they stole my car, did they?"

I nodded.

He smiled and nodded. "Guess I better file a report with the cops then, huh?"

I nodded again, wondering when he would snap out of it and start pounding the crap out of me. But the longer he sat there, the more I felt something was crazy wrong. I wondered if I should be looking for the signs of a stroke or something. None of this made any sense. But then again, my life rarely did.

"Nobody you ever seen here in my place, were they? The kidnappers, I mean?"

I shook my head.

"Good. That's real good, Bailey." He took another swig. "Come 'ere." He held an arm open.

I took a tentative step forward, uncertain whether I should expect a fondling or a beating. He reached out the rest of the way, reeled me in, and patted my butt affectionately.

"I'm glad to hear it, Bailey," he said.

I finally asked it out loud, eyebrow raised. "Are you okay?"

"Had a bit to drink," he said. "I was worried."

"About your car?"

He laughed. "Yeah. About my car." He swatted my rear again. "Now you go clock in."

I was relieved to get out of that room—and stunned that I'd gotten off without a beating. Still, my heart was pounding. I couldn't make heads or tails out of what had just happened. So I simply penciled made-up hours onto my time card, tied on my apron, slipped past Jimmy as fast as possible, and hit the floor.

CHAPTER TWELVE
JIMMY

Jimmy shoved his glasses up his nose and watched Bailey as she hurried into the dining room, tying her apron strings over her pert *glutei maximi*. They were curvilinear in just the right degree so as to provoke hormonal reactions in adolescent males—such as himself. The effects were not unpleasant. In fact, they brought to mind a number of experiments he wouldn't mind running with her...

None of which he'd ever run before, but that was beside the point.

She was what common folk would refer to, colloquially, as "hot," though she did not fall under the same classification as their classmate Michaela Stewart. Michaela was destined for the fashion runway no doubt—and that was all her brains were good for, expending her full concentration towards balancing on pinpoint heels while swinging her hips provocatively and applying another layer of lip gloss. Granted, she did play a competitive round of tennis.

Bailey, conversely, was more like the cute girl down the street, and even if she wasn't a genius, at least she was good in school. They said she got A's in almost every class.

Genius would have been more attractive, but it was perversely hard to come by. Jimmy should know. None of the kids at Badger High were his equal when it came to brains. In fact, in his studied opinion, neither were the teachers.

Jimmy threw a consortium of kitchen cutlery, freshly cleaned, into a giant kettle for easy transport and hauled it all into the kitchen. He shoved knives into drawers and hung ladles above the stove.

He'd gone to the nth degree all last semester to discover the correct combination of courtship rituals that would win Bailey's attention, but she remained stubbornly disinterested. Turning down a private and massively exclusive invitation to his scientific lab had been the lowest blow yet. Despite their intellectual disparity, they were nearly the same in height and weight, and equally outcast from society, which statistically made them a good match. Furthermore, her good looks would only enhance his carefree appearance as a man who devoted his time to learning and science, not fashion.

He used the sleeve of his tee shirt, still damp with dishwater and hanging below his elbow, to scrub away the reddish-brown ring stuck to the rim of the kettle. He grinned. Much better. He threw the kettle on a shelf and stalked confidently back to his soapy domain.

Never before had he invited someone to his secret lab—and she'd had the audacity to turn him down. Didn't she realize the honor? He would have shown her his groundbreaking experiments—stuff that would land him in history books someday. She would have been beside herself with awe. She would have begged to know more about every detail—and he would gladly have enlightened her.

All those hours she spent at the library, her nose in a book... had he mistakenly believed she was a fellow intellectual?

No. He was never wrong. She was merely playing hard-to-get. Didn't females play little games like that? How obnoxious.

He scraped limp veggies and dried gravy into the trash and lined up the dishes on the plastic tray.

He'd show her. He'd show everyone what a genius he was. And then Bailey would regret turning him away.

The bomb was almost ready.

CHAPTER THIRTEEN
BUD

Bud finished off the whiskey and tossed the empty bottle into a corner of the room, where it crashed into a pile of other empty bottles and cans. Somewhere beneath that mess, there used to be a garbage bin—the little type people put in fancy-ass powder rooms. It had a friggin' bird on the side and the whole bit. Or was it a flower? He couldn't remember. It had been too long since he'd seen it. Happily, the empty containers weren't all from today. He'd be wasted if they were.

Haha. He *was* wasted.

Reaching unsteadily across his desk, he grabbed his cell phone. When he flopped back into his chair, it nearly tipped over and dumped him out. He muttered under his breath and tried to focus on the phone screen. After he finally found the call app, he chicken pecked at the numbers. He had to backspace a few times, and eventually just started over fresh. Finally, he got the number in and hit the call button.

The other line picked up almost immediately. "Well?" The Man was eager.

"Hey, handsome."

There was a pause. "Are you *drunk?*"

"What else would I be?"

"It's two in the afternoon."

"It's five o'clock somewhere." Bud laughed and belched.

"Is there a point to this conversation, or are you simply dialing people at random?"

"Hey, man, don't get your shit in a twist." That wasn't the right expression, was it? Hell. "I got news. We don't gotta worry about Bailey."

"Is that so?" His tone was unconvinced.

"She don't know nuthin'."

"And how did you conclude that?"

"I asked her."

"You didn't..." He sounded as if he were about to have a heart attack. "Weber, what did you tell her?"

"That I was there? Hell, no! What do you think I am, stupid?"

The silence on the other end of the line dragged out a little too long. Disgruntled, Bud sat up and grabbed an empty beer bottle to fidget with.

"Look, all I had to do was ask what happened to my car. She spilled everything. I flat-out asked her if she recognized the guy who got away—you know? So I could find out who the frick was kidnapping my customers. Know what I mean?" He fumbled the beer bottle, sending it over the edge of the desk. "I'm tellin' ya, she ate the whole thing. She don't have a clue it was me."

"I suppose I'll just have to take your word for that."

"Aw, c'mon, man, what do I gotta do to convince you?"

"Quite frankly, there is nothing."

"Crap. I suppose I shouldn'ta called you drunk."

"It would have helped your cause. Did you dispose of your car?"

"It's in the bottom of a lake somewhere."

"Where?"

"Dude, *I* don't even know. I've been drunk ever since."
He laughed. "I don't even remember how I got home."

There was an audible sigh. "Very well, then."

"So what you got for me to do now?"

"Nothing. I need to rework the plan. I didn't foresee
that we'd have to get Fritz and Jason out of the way. I
thought they'd be on board. I was counting on them."

Homie wasn't as brilliant as he pretended to be, in
other words. Bud smirked, but quickly wiped it away. "Hey,
man, you still got me," he said, trying to sound genuine and
concerned. "I can do whatever you want." Despite losing a
car to the cause, The Man was still good business. If Bud
had known he could make this kind of money, he never
would have worked his butt off running a bar.

"I appreciate your enthusiasm, Weber, but there's
nothing to be done now. The situation is too hot. I need you
to lay low for now."

"All right, all right, all right, sure," Bud mumbled,
nodding.

"Call me if anything changes—especially if Bailey
remembers you were there."

"Wow, you're, like, obsessed with that."

"Weber—"

"Okay, okay, I got it."

"Good." The line went dead.

Bud threw his phone down. Bastard couldn't even
spare a good-bye. But his orders were clear. Sit. Wait. Do
nothing.

He smirked.

He had other plans. He had a certain score to settle.

SUNDAY
JUNE 22, 2014

CHAPTER FOURTEEN
ROLAND

Roland Markham drew his knife through rind and yellow pulp, making a pile of lemon rings on his cutting board, each slice glistening in tart juice. As he dropped the rings into a pitcher of iced tea, glowing in morning sunlight, he couldn't help but feel a little lonely. It had only been two days since a policeman had knocked on his door in the middle of the night, bearing the news.

Roland gave the iced tea a swirl with a long spoon. This had been their tradition—his and Charles'—going back to the days when the kitchen had been filled with the chatter of their wives as they prepared the refreshments and the laughter of the children as they ran through the house in bare feet and swimsuits.

The years had turned, the children had grown and scattered, Charles had divorced, and Roland's wife had passed on. But as the two men had turned old and found themselves alone and with fewer commitments, they had gravitated back toward their tradition.

Even though things had only become increasingly awkward.

Charles had been dreaming. Had been for as long as they'd known each other. Roland was straight as the day was long—that was all there was to it. As it was, Charles' hopeful advances had accomplished nothing but to put them both at risk. There would have been a scandal if anyone had found out. Neither man's career would have survived.

It was ironic, really, that they'd remained friends at all. Inexplicable. For the sake of appearances—maybe even for the sake of old friendship—they had both mastered the art of ignoring the elephant in the room. Or at least Roland had.

But now Charles was gone. Dead. A casualty of those very dreams. The man had been convinced, apparently, that he could finally win Roland's devotion by seeking revenge for the death of Roland's son, so many years ago. But who, after all, was really to blame? Fritz and Jason, for leading Bobby astray? Or Wade Erickson, for firing the bullet that had killed him? Or was there anyone to blame at all?

How much responsibility was due to Roland himself?

He sighed, leaning on the counter, and dwelt on the harrowing possibility that he had never even known his own son. Had missed Bobby's entire boyhood. His entire adulthood, brief as it had been. How much had Roland himself become like his own father? And his grandfather before him? Always tied up at *The Bank*. Always away in *The City*. Roland's life had become an endless ream of figures, zero through nine, in various combinations, punctuated only by commas, decimals, and dollar signs.

And somewhere between the bundles of cold, hard cash, a boy had become a man... and died. Died in an illicit pursuit of the very thing the Markhams apparently loved so dearly: cash. Died alone, perhaps, even surrounded as he was by his partners in crime, Jason and Fritz.

Yes, Bobby had died very much alone.

Roland rinsed the knife and cutting board under a stream of water, then stowed them in a rack in the dishwasher and dried his hands on a towel. Well, Charles had accomplished what he'd set out to do. Fritz and Jason were dead, the both of them.

Fritz had no parents left to mourn his loss.

But Roland didn't have to stretch his imagination far to know what Tommy felt now.

You could never look at your own children, whatever sins they may have committed, without picturing the little ones they had once been. So small. So perfect. So full of promise. Their death was a pain that never dulled—simply became crusted over, the way an oyster tries to bury a grain of sand. A hundred layers later, you think you've distanced yourself. You tell yourself that the jagged edges are polished over and can't hurt you anymore. That the memories have even become beautiful.

But in reality, you've only made the problem bigger. Worse. It's taken up more and more space. And in the process, it's pushed out everything else. It's pinched the nerves. Cut off the blood flow. Left you numb. You've forgotten how to feel. How to feel anything at all.

Roland sighed and gazed through the window above the sink, stretching his eyes across his spacious lawn sloping down to the lake. He tried to soak in the reality of Charles' death. He tried to feel the pain, if there was any there to be felt, buried under all the layers of pearl.

There wasn't. It was a hard adjustment for an old man to suddenly drink his iced tea alone. That vaguely morose thought was the best he could muster.

Roland gradually became aware that he hadn't merely been staring out his window, but was in fact watching a boy stroll down the Lake Shore Path, coming from the direction of town. Perhaps *stroll* wasn't the right word. He slinked, shoulders rolled inward, head on the swivel. The boy could hardly have weighed more than a hundred pounds and was practically drowning in a tee shirt that could have been re-purposed as a sail. Over his shoulder, he carried a backpack.

Much to Roland's surprise, the lad jumped the gate to his pier.

Still glancing to and fro, the boy dashed about half-way down the dock, then pulled up short and carefully divested himself of the backpack. He laid it on the boards and, as naturally as if he were swimming off his own pier, he slid into the lake. Holding on to one of the pier posts, he reached up to the bag and removed a small cylindrical object from the interior, roughly the size of a flashlight. Puzzled, Roland watched for several more moments as the boy appeared to attach the item to the underside of the pier.

What sort of mischief was this, then? Frowning furiously, Roland made for the door, only to draw up short on the threshold.

On second thought, he should bring the tea.

He returned to the counter, dropped in a sprig of mint, and grabbed the pitcher along with a pair of drinking glasses.

CHAPTER FIFTEEN
JIMMY

———— ⛭ ————

Submerged in lake water, up to his arm pits, Jimmy re-adjusted his leg lock on the pier post under Roland Markham's dock. The wooden post was slick with algae and felt disgusting against his bare calves. He choked back his revulsion and concentrated on his task: wiring a small, remotely-operated bomb to the underside of the pier.

It was a simple affair—he could build a dozen of them in his sleep—but powerful enough to obliterate the pier, the classic wooden power boat, and the antique steam yacht in an almighty show of supreme power, cunning, and intellect.

This was where the first body had been found—what's-his-name. Fritz Geissler. The local news outlets were reporting on a second killing just the other night, leaving two dead and a third flown. The scenario was ideal for Jimmy's purposes. The cops would think their wanted man had returned to the scene of the crime to destroy some bit of evidence they'd overlooked.

When Jimmy was ready to reveal himself, they would know the truth: that they had much bigger problems on their hands than a rogue murderer.

The buzz of a power boat zoomed closer. Jimmy ducked, the water lapping at his chin. The boat veered past, music blaring, the occupants dancing on the deck in swimsuits, waving their arms in the air.

Idiots. If they'd come by ten minutes from now, they would have been blown to bits. His face warmed in vindictive fury and he scowled holes into the hull of their boat.

He didn't see the wake until it hit him full in the face and washed over his head. It passed, and he sputtered water out of his nose and mouth while rivulets ran down his glasses. He flipped them the bird.

Hugging the slimy post as if he were one of his own pre-historic, tree-dwelling ancestors, he used his pliers to put a few last twists on the wires holding his little creation in place. Satisfied that it wasn't going to slip off into the lake, he set his tools on the pier. Once he was out of the water and his tools were packed, he'd set the timer and flick on the arming switch. He grabbed the edge of the pier to hoist himself up.

"Good afternoon, young man."

Jimmy gawked up into the round, smiling face of the very subject he had selected for this glorious moment: Roland Markham, CEO (ret.) of Chicago International Bank, President (past) of the National League of Bank Executives, primary and sole dweller of Markwood Estate on Geneva Lake, south shore. He carried a pitcher of iced tea, swirling with ice cubes and thin slices of lemon.

"Have you lost something?" the old man asked.

"What? No." Jimmy pushed his glasses up his nose and glanced at his bomb, hoping Markham couldn't see it.

"Oh. You fell in?"

"Uh... yeah. I fell in."

"Well, that's bound to happen now and again, particularly on a gated and locked pier where the public aren't allowed. Did you realize the gate was locked?" He motioned casually towards the white picket gate at the head of the pier. Such gates were common around the lake and served to remind walkers on the Lake Shore Path that the piers were private property.

"Uh..."

"Oh, I'm sure you noticed. Why else would you have jumped over it?"

Despite his recent drink of lake water, Jimmy's mouth went dry. How long had this old geezer been watching him? What should he do? He was caught red-handed. He could detonate the bomb now, with the old man standing there...

"You seem to have been working on something very fastidiously down there," Markham babbled on. Then, much to Jimmy's horror, the old man creakily got to his knees, set the pitcher on the edge of the pier, and leaned over the brink, nearly hanging upside-down. "Ohhh, what have we here? That looks quite professional. A bomb, am I right?"

Jimmy merely gaped at him, hardly believing this conversation was happening.

The man went on. "Not that explosives are my forte, but I wager you have a quality piece of equipment here. It isn't possible you built this yourself?"

"What if I did?" Jimmy sneered.

"I'd be mightily impressed! You're an aficionado?"

Aficionado? He wanted to blurt that he was an effing prodigy. It nearly leapt out, too, but he bit his tongue just in time. He was in enough trouble already.

As if reading his thoughts, the old man sat back on his heels and flapped his hand. "Oh, come, come, come. I was just paying you a compliment. I'll tell you what. I won't say a thing about this if you don't blow it up. Hmm? What say you? Can we come to terms?"

Markham didn't seem the least bit concerned that he was literally sitting on top of a bomb. The old fool had guts, Jimmy had to give him that.

"I'll sweeten the deal," Markham continued. "I'd like to hear how you made it. I've always had a taste for diverse knowledge, and can you believe? I've lived over seventy years, and I still don't know how a bomb is made."

Jimmy realized he'd been slipping down the pier post again. He hiked himself up and pushed his glasses up his nose. "You won't tell anyone?"

The old man pursed his lips, frowned, and shook his head vigorously. "Not a soul."

Jimmy chewed on that. His choices were two: Humor the old geezer, or blow them both up. He decided this wasn't the exit he'd spent sleepless nights savoring. He didn't want that moment to be a snap decision. He wanted to relish it.

He reached up to the ledge for his pliers and began to unwind the wires he'd secured a moment ago. The old man smiled his approval.

As the device came loose and slid down the post, Markham shot his hand out to catch it. "Careful, don't want to lose it. I suppose water damages these things?"

"Well, if it's a waterproof bomb, it wouldn't matter." Jimmy couldn't help boasting.

"Oh, is this one waterproof?"

"No."

"But I'm sure you know how to make one."

"Haven't tried yet, but I understand the principles. I'm confident I could produce a functioning model."

The old man smiled. "I have no doubt."

When the last wire was cut, Markham cradled the bomb in both hands as if it were a wounded bird and cautiously got to his feet. Whipping out a white handkerchief, he nestled the bomb in the monogrammed fabric. Meanwhile, Jimmy pulled himself out of the water, his clothes dripping and his shoes sloshing.

"I'm Roland, by the way." The old man offered his palm.

"Duh," Jimmy replied with a shrug. He ignored the handshake and proceeded to wring water out of his tee shirt.

Instead of taking offense, the millionaire simply grinned. "And your name is…?"

"Oppenheimer."

Markham's eyebrows jumped high. "Oppenheimer! Inventor of the atomic bomb. You take your art seriously, young man."

Jimmy tried to toss his bangs nonchalantly. Wet hair slapped him across the face and plastered itself across his eyes.

Markham moved toward a collection of deck furniture and nodded to the pitcher he'd left on the pier. "Bring that iced tea over, will you, ah… Jimmy?"

Jimmy gaped. "How did you—?" He caught himself and straightened his spine. "Who's Jimmy?"

Markham pointed towards his feet. "I assume 'Jimmy' would be whoever owns that cap."

Jimmy glanced down at his baseball cap, parked upside down next to his tools. During a particularly bad hat-stealing epidemic at school two years ago, he had inscribed his own name with indelible ink across the inside of the band. Crap.

The old man winked and sat down at the wooden table and chairs, painted white to match the pier.

Jimmy grabbed up the pitcher and thunked it down on the table. Plopping into a chair, he tried drying his glasses on his tee shirt, but only succeeded in swirling the water around.

Markham pulled out his own pair of spectacles from a pocket in his loose-fitting cardigan. He put them on with one hand, still balancing the bomb in the handkerchief in his other hand. "Detonated by a time mechanism, I see?"

"Yep." Jimmy shoved his glasses back on and stared through the water specks.

"How powerful is it?"

"Your pier would be history," Jimmy said simply.

Markham bobbed a finger at the device. "You really built this yourself?"

Jimmy nodded. "Yes, sir."

"It's genius."

Jimmy sat a little taller and puffed his chest out.

"This isn't your first, is it?"

"I've built dozens."

"Dozens?" Markham's eyes went wide. "What do you do with them?"

"Experiment. I know an abandoned field. I took down an old barn that used to be there. Took me a few tries, but I got 'er in the end."

"But this was your first try on property that was still in use?"

"Well... yeah, I guess."

Markham laid the bomb down on the table, still cushioned in his handkerchief, and filled two glasses of tea from the pitcher. Ice cubes and lemon slices tumbled over the lip. "Well, and to what do I owe this honor?"

"This is where they found that body," Jimmy replied. He pointed to the glass sitting in front of him. "Is this sweet?"

"It is."

Jimmy grabbed it in both hands and chugged it down. Hell, yeah, it was good and sweet.

"And you figured they'd peg it on the murderer?" the old man went on.

Jimmy set the empty glass down with a clunk and wiped his mouth on the back of his hand. "Yep. Cleaning up his crime scene. Pretty smart, huh?"

"Would my flagpole have remained intact?" Markham motioned over his shoulder.

Jimmy looked across the yard. A flagpole was centered in the yard near the head of the pier. "Eh, probably." Jimmy tossed back the last drop in the bottom of the glass, wondering why the old man cared about his flagpole more than his pier and boats. Patriotic sort?

"Oh. In that case, yes, your plan isn't bad. But you'll observe, I do have a security camera overlooking my pier."

Jimmy looked again. Beneath the U.S. flag, a black, orb-like eye stared down at them. Crap. "You're not going to...?"

"Show the footage to the police? Certainly not. I gave my word."

Jimmy allowed himself to slouch. He eyed his empty glass and the half-full pitcher.

Markham grinned and topped him off, then leaned back in his chair. "Why were you going to do it?"

Jimmy paused with the glass half-way to his mouth. What should he say? How much should he tell? How much should he lie?

Markham folded his hands in his lap and shrugged with his thumbs. "Most people who set off bombs have some sort of message to convey. What was your message? Who was it for? Was there something you were trying to tell *me?*"

Jimmy set his glass back down and rubbed behind his ear. "No."

"My pier was simply convenient, because a dead body was found there?"

Jimmy nodded.

"What else? What do you want the world to know?"

Jimmy hated open-ended questions. He let the silence linger for an uncomfortably long time, hoping the old man would be the first to break. But he seemed content to sit in his chair until he died and his bones bleached.

Jimmy's throat tightened as a lifetime of resentment flashed across his memory. The pressure built inside until he wished he *had* detonated the bomb.

"They all hate me," he finally blurted.

"Who does?"

72

"Everyone. The other kids bully me around. Humiliate me in front of everyone."

Last spring, someone had put a note in his locker, telling him to meet Michaela by the main doors after his last class. Michaela's name was signed at the bottom, and the sticky note was covered in little hearts. He'd been Johnny-on-the-spot, and when Michaela had walked out the doors, surrounded by her flock of popular girls, all of them aglow with pink and glitter, he'd strutted right up to her, grinning, then stood there like an idiot, waiting for her to speak first.

She'd eyed him up and down with a look of disgust and asked him if he had a problem.

He showed her the note.

She read it, looked him up and down a few more times, shook her head as if clearing an offensive aroma from her olfactory nerves, then simply brushed past him, her gaggle giggling in her wake.

Half the school had been standing there.

Jimmy felt his face warming again at the memory. He twisted the glass of iced tea back and forth, grinding it into the table. "They don't know who they're messing with. They're all a bunch of idiots. One day, they'll all be assimilated into the world, faceless nobodies whose existence doesn't even matter. But not me. No one knows me now. But they will. I'll be the greatest scientist of our age. I'll make discoveries and inventions no one ever dreamed of. Those kids who bully me today? *Their* kids will learn about me in school. My name will be right there alongside Einstein and Oppenheimer. I'm going to win the Nobel Prize in Physics. People will boast I was a local boy. There'll be a plaque in one of the parks—maybe even a statue. They'll try to forget everything they did to me. But I won't. I'll remember it. All of it."

Markham nodded slowly. "I see. And this bomb—?" he pointed to the device on the table. "This bomb will help you win the Nobel?"

Jimmy flushed even hotter. If the old man was making fun of him…

Markham leaned back in his chair and regarded him thoughtfully. "I believe you, young man. I believe you have it in you to accomplish everything you set your mind to. You remind me of my grandfather—a man with a dream and little more. He came to this part of the country without two dimes to rub together. But he had a goal, he kept it at the center of his mind, and he worked hard. Three generations later, his dream is now one of the largest banks in America. The reward of his labors sits on the hill behind us." He motioned toward the pillared mansion on the manicured lawn, its grandeur enough to inspire jealousy in the President of the United States. "I see that same fire in you, young man. But it needs shaping. It needs direction." He pointed at the bomb again. "This? This won't get you a Nobel."

Jimmy jiggled his foot and scowled. "What will?"

Markham leaned forward and whispered. "A *plan*."

CHAPTER SIXTEEN
JIMMY

After stowing his unused and deactivated bomb in his secret lab—once known as the garden shed—Jimmy entered his house through the rear door. The screen slammed behind him and nearly fell off its hinges. The screws attaching them to the door frame were so loose, it was only a matter of time. He calculated a 90% probability of the screen succumbing to atrophy within the next four to six weeks. That came down to as many as 418 operations, or 104.5 uses per family member, counting both his parents and his snobby older sister, but skipping the chinchilla, who had no use for doors, despite having evolved opposable thumbs. No one ever bothered to fix the screen, and no one ever would, even after it eventually fell clean off. It would lie on the porch however it landed, and everyone who came and went would simply step over it, until, perhaps, one day his father would kick it half-way across the yard in an alcohol-induced emotional state.

Jimmy was starving. He crossed the kitchen, pulled open the fridge door, and stuck his head inside. The shelves were crammed full, and his choices were varied. Cheese, moldy. Soda, near-empty. Somebody's left-over hamburger, soggy. He finally found a bowl of jello salad with marshmallows. Divine. In the figurative sense, of course.

He grabbed the bowl, peeled back the wrapping, stuck his fingers in, and licked them off. Who'd made this? Clearly not his mother.

"James Aldridge Beacon!"

Speaking of whom...

He looked up. His mother stormed into the kitchen. Her hair, the color of dishwater, hung haphazardly in her face, and her chest, bra-less, sagged inside her tank top.

"Look at this mess!"

To which did she refer? His eyes traveled from the table, piled with unpaid bills, to the counter, cluttered with a disassembled toaster oven, to the sink, overflowing with dishes. Any one of them fit the description provided, including his mother herself.

"I fail to comprehend to which—"

"Quit talking like a goddamn professor. *Look*." She pointed at the floor.

His soggy shoes had left an unmistakable trail through the layer of dirt on the linoleum, turning his footprints to mud. And her point was?

"What have you been up to?" she demanded.

"Experimenting."

She folded her arms, as saggy as every other part of her body. "Oh, and what set-up were you testing this time? A dunking tank at the fair?"

Her jibe stung. But he would never let *her* know that. He lifted his chin. "As a matter of fact, the nature of my experiments are, in general, on such a superior level to the brainpower of the average individual that I doubt many could attain to it, much less a specimen of your feeble intelligence."

She furrowed her brow at him. "Did you just dis your own mother?"

Jimmy placed his hand over his heart while mocking a gasp. "The subject is cognizant! A groundbreaking discovery."

She stormed forward and grabbed him by the ear. Jimmy let out a yelp and dropped the bowl. Pink jello salad sprayed across the linoleum and splattered his legs.

"Now look what you've done," his mother bellowed. "You are going to your room this instant, young man!"

He attempted to beg for mercy—or at least the release of his ear—but to no avail. His mother escorted him all the way to his room, shoved him in, and slammed the door. The lock snicked shut from the outside. His mother had installed a doorknob backwards specifically so she could dispose of her son at will. It had been his fourteenth birthday present—only, he was sure his mother had forgotten it had been his birthday.

He rubbed his ear until circulation returned, then crashed into the chair behind his desk and pulled out a pencil and a sheet of paper. The lock didn't matter. His mother seemed to have overlooked the idea that Jimmy could simply climb out the window—a fact which merely led weight to Jimmy's argument regarding his mother's intelligence.

Jimmy licked the tip of his pencil. Thanks to his conversation with the elderly millionaire, he now had a new experiment to design.

Searching for inspiration, he cast his gaze around the walls and the many scientific displays that adorned them. A periodic table of the elements. A hanging model of the solar system. Artists' glowing representations of an atom, light waves, and the multiverse. A marker board the size of a plate glass window crammed with equations in his own handwriting. Any remaining sections of blank wall were adorned with posters featuring the greatest minds of the centuries. Galileo. Edison. Einstein. These were his true peers. A lesser mind like his mother's would simply never understand. But here he was, trapped, a fish suffocating in an unnatural, unforgiving environment.

Roland Markham had said that all Jimmy needed was a plan, and had proceeded to expound upon the value of drafting an outline of one's own life-to-come, complete with career goals, financial goals, personal goals, logical steps to achieve all of the above, and deadlines by which all should be accomplished.

Jimmy leaned over his page and scribed a title: *The Master Plan of J. A. Beacon.* After a moment's thought, he added a subtitle: *A Pre-Autobiography.* Brilliant.

First, to graduate high school as soon as possible. He would find a way to escape the local public institution and get into a private school for accelerated learners. In such an environment, he expected he could polish off his diploma within the next twelve months—a full year ahead of his fellow students. It pained him that he clearly could have had his diploma by now, had his parents only realized he was being suffocated in classrooms designed for the ordinary masses.

Next, college. He had his eye on the physics program at Harvard. He expected he could claim his bachelor's degree in a matter of two or three years, his master's in another twelve months. His doctorate couldn't possibly take more than three or four years. He chewed his eraser and stared at the wall. It was very likely he'd have his Nobel Prize by then, as well. He jotted this all down, then proceeded to financial goals. A multi-million-dollar mansion on the lake by the age of twenty-five didn't seem out of his reach...

As his dreams took shape, with its long list of honors, degrees, and accomplishments, Jimmy cast his eye over the page with approval. Surely, this plan would propel him to the life of greatness he'd always known should be his. The mere sight of it on paper made it feel more real. More attainable.

But if not, there was always his alternate plan. The Backfire Model. The Backfire had nothing to do with the diminutive bomb he'd tied to Roland Markham's pier. That was only ever meant to be the precursor—the foreword before the textbook, the orchestra warming up before the concert. And while he'd diagrammed the Backfire itself—long ago—he'd never fully laid out his plans for how or when to detonate it. The whole idea was more of a fancy in the back of his mind. But he did like to toy with it.

Should he outline his plan for the unveiling of the Backfire, as well? Just in case *The Master Plan* failed?

He put his pencil away. Perhaps not. At least, perhaps not yet.

He threw himself into the pile of blankets and pillows on his bed, nestled his head in his folded hands, and gazed again at his posters. He met the black-and-white, glossy-finished gaze of his true hero, J. Robert Oppenheimer. This man had been the genius behind the most powerful force of physics the world had ever witnessed, the atomic bomb, only eclipsed in more recent years by its progeny, the hydrogen bomb. A brilliant mind, Oppenheimer, though he had eventually abhorred his own creation. Like Frankenstein did his monster. Like Jimmy was despised by his mother.

Across the bottom of the poster, Jimmy had scrawled Oppenheimer's most famous quote. Granted, it had its first origins in a religious text, the *Bhagavad Gita*. But they had been made famous by the mouth of the great physicist.

I am become Death, the destroyer of worlds.

Somehow, the words had always resonated with Jimmy.

MONDAY
JUNE 23, 2014

CHAPTER SEVENTEEN
MONICA

The great goal of many on a Monday morning is to drag their carcass to work half alive and roughly on time. I have no sympathy for such people. On this particular Monday, my only motivation was to get back to my office pronto—but without being spotted. Especially by the chief.

The weekend was over and the tourists had migrated back to Chicago and elsewhere, leaving the streets of Lake Geneva easy to navigate once again. Still, I tapped my steering wheel impatiently while strategizing how to get into the police department and up to my office. If I came in through the main doors instead of the employee entrance, I'd only have to slip past the telecommunicators behind the public service window. Half the time, our staff on the other side of the mic were buried in phone calls and radio traffic. I could breeze past them, then a flight of stairs would take me directly to my office—my fuzzy gray cubicle—and I would be home free.

The chief had made it clear I was to take a long weekend. And I think it was safe to say I had. I'd run errands, cleaned the house, re-arranged the furniture, mowed the lawn, trimmed the hedges, changed the oil in my car, re-painted a room, and even fit in my daily jog. I had too much steam built up to sit around and do nothing.

And despite all that, I could think of nothing but the Wall and its cataclysmic collapse at the hands of a teenage girl. She had left me vulnerable and exposed in a way I hadn't felt in years.

About the time I'd begun to consider a complete remodel of the guest bathroom, I realized I was running out of projects to distract me at home. So I was running the gauntlet and sneaking back into work.

Charles Hart's missing accomplice bothered me—and not just because we had no leads as to his identity or whereabouts. The more I thought about the case, the more I knew in my gut that we had no idea what we were dealing with.

I breathed deeply, letting the clean lake air revitalize my brain cells. The smell of the hunt was a refreshing brew; the stress of the chase, a drug that both fed and starved my soul.

I pulled into the parking lot outside the PD, grabbed my portfolio off the passenger seat, and made tracks for the front door.

"Monica?"

I stopped and crunched my eyes shut. Damn it, I hadn't even made it inside the building yet. Sighing, I turned to face whoever had busted me. I caught an eyeful of sculpted pectorals showing through a snug black tee shirt. Ryan Brandt. I scowled. It pained me that I still knew my ex by his muscle mass. I would have been happier if he'd turned flabby and bald over the past ten years. Not because I was still attracted to him in any way, because I assure you, I was *not*. I simply craved his utter downfall in all areas of life.

I glanced over his shoulder at his car—a sleek, black two-door with four interlaced circles glittering across the grill. I hoisted an eyebrow. "Audi. Really?" The contrast of this particular set of wheels to a cop currently working bike patrol was too much.

He worked his jaw, but his eyes were obscured behind blue-tinted sunglasses. He shrugged and dropped the keys he'd been twirling into his jeans pocket. "I got a good deal on it used." As if to quickly change the subject, he shoved his hands into his back pockets. "I thought you had the day off?"

"I thought *you* did," I shot back. The snark had returned. Nothing like a little taste of Ryan Brandt to put the Wall back in place. Security systems up and activated. Weapons locked and loaded. It was good to be back.

He motioned towards the building. "Just thought I'd pump some iron in the gym."

I let my eyes flicker up and down his buff figure and shifted an eyebrow. "Yeah, I think you'd better."

Shit. My sarcasm was showing. He belonged in advertisements for things like whiskey, cologne, and men's briefs. Every time he walked into a bar, mini-skirted hopefuls slipped in their own drool just to win a glance from him. The worst part was, he knew it. Played it. Embraced it. With a stab to the gut, I reminded myself that my ex was nothing but a womanizer. I flipped open the portfolio in my hand, turned, and continued toward the door, my nostrils flaring. Damn, it felt good to put him down.

"Um..." Ryan muttered, for once in his life at a loss for words.

I spun. "Nothing," I said with a dramatic shrug, arms spread. I was riding this bitch wave all the way to the end. "I meant nothing. Why do you always think I'm on your back?" But of course, I *was*. On purpose. Because I could. Stupid Wall.

His brows wavered. "I didn't say—"

I snapped the portfolio shut and planted a hand on my hip. "So, have you applied for a permanent position here yet?" Despite his twenty years of experience in law enforcement, he was currently only employed in a temporary job, pedaling two wheels around the tourist district. Why he'd given up his rank as a sergeant in Minneapolis for a rookie position, I couldn't fathom. It only underscored the already pathetic image he cut in my mind. But like the other rookies, he'd be out of a job by the end of the summer when the tourists went home and the workload dropped drastically. I couldn't wait.

"No, I haven't applied," he said.

"I thought you wanted to stay."

"There aren't any openings."

"Really?" I smiled sweetly, like a cupcake with too much frosting. "That's too bad."

Ryan ducked his head and rubbed the back of his neck—the way he did when he was starting to lose his patience, but trying not to.

There she was again—my inner bitch. She'd been the defining element of my character ever since Ryan had cheated on me. I hadn't always been like this. But I couldn't remember what I'd been like before. That version of me had died a long time ago, and this piece of crap was what had come to take her place.

I was on the verge of walking away again when Ryan stopped me.

"Monica, I was wondering about that necklace—the one Jason Thomlin gave to Bailey. When are you going to release it?"

I shrugged. "I haven't verified its role in the investigation yet."

"Then you haven't proved that it had anything to do with the commission of a crime. I already talked with Lehman. It's been photographed. Logged. Noted in the documentation. There's no real value to it."

I looked at him through slitted eyes. "Why is this a big deal?"

His gaze dropped, like a bad card shark checking his hand. Whatever Brandt saw in that hand, he apparently decided to lay it all out on the table. He met my eye again. "Jason meant for her to have it," he said simply.

I snarked out loud. This was unreal. I knew Brandt was strangely protective of the kid Bailey, but did he seriously expect me to compromise an investigation just for nostalgia? "I refuse to underestimate anything connected to this case," I retorted. "For all we know, two murders could hinge on a necklace."

Brandt spread his hands. "You have no proof that it was involved in the commission of a crime. So you have no grounds for keeping it. It's a charm. You can buy one for five bucks at Walmart."

I raised a snide eyebrow. "Then get her one from Walmart."

"Monica." He sighed and closed his eyes momentarily. His next word appeared to pain him. "Please?"

"Oh, well, if you say the magic word."

"Then you'll release it?"

"When I've had time to look into it." I lifted my portfolio. "I have a million things to do, Brandt. So take a number."

He rolled his eyes and growled under his breath, then turned and strode toward the employee entrance.

I straightened my shoulders, feeling a little better. The Wall was back, and the bitch was in.

I probably shouldn't have been proud of that.

CHAPTER EIGHTEEN
RYAN

I shoved my way through the door into the gym, still steaming. The last time Monica and I had talked, she'd been almost warm—as warm as she ever got with me these days. And now, apparently, we were back to her factory preset. I must have bumped the wrong button, but I wasn't sure which one it was, or how to fix it.

Something snapped me on the back of the legs.

My body tensed and I whirled. A grinning Mike Schultz, one of the patrol officers, stood behind the door, twirling a towel and snickering like a school boy.

"God, Schultz!" I gasped—probably more dramatically than the situation called for.

"Bro," he laughed, ducking back and holding up the towel like a shield, "I guess I'd better not try that when you're armed."

I took a slow breath and forced myself to loosen up. "Sorry. I guess I've been a little jumpy lately." Specifically, ever since I'd nearly been gunned down in the street a few nights ago. But I'd been trying not to dwell on that, afraid the automatic replay might take root like a volunteer tree that refused to die, no matter how many times you ran it over with the mower.

I pulled my tee shirt up over my head. I'd planned on a light workout, but after the exchange of gunfire with Monica in the parking lot, I was ready to work up a sweat. "Warmed up the equipment for me?" I asked.

He slung the towel around his shoulders. "I put sand in all the moving parts."

"Ha-ha. Very funny."

"Dude, you're purple."

I glanced down at my chest. Three slugs had hammered into the trauma plate of my body armor that night. The Kevlar had saved my bacon and left me with these multicolored mementos. I rubbed at them, as if I could wipe them away, but the ache told me they'd be around for a while. "It's looking better, believe it or not."

"God, I thought you were a goner. That was some shit."

I grimaced and turned my attention to the bench press, wishing Schultz would quit talking about it. I was doing my best to push the whole thing out of my mind. A picture kept flashing through my head of an active shooter scenario... people falling, helpless... and me just standing there like an idiot, frozen to the spot, obsessed with my own mortality.

I slapped my shirt down on the seat of the bench press, grabbed a forty-five–pound disc, and slammed it onto the bar.

"Hey, are we cool?" Schultz's voice wavered with nerves. "I'm sorry, Brandt. I was trying to cover you, I swear to God. I was a bit slow on the uptake, I admit it. But man, it just came out of nowhere. I'm sorry."

A pang jabbed me in the chest. I hadn't meant for him to think I was mad at him. Truth be told, I couldn't have testified whether Mike had hesitated, or charged into the gunfire screaming like a banshee and wielding a pair of rocket launchers. I'd been flat on the pavement myself, staring into a street lamp, completely dazed. He hadn't hesitated nearly as long as I had.

"God, I unloaded a whole magazine," Mike sputtered on, wringing the ends of his towel as it hung over his neck. "I can't believe I never hit him. I promise, I passed my last firearms qualification, but shit. It's not like the paper print-out at the shooting range, man. I don't know what got into me—"

I held up a hand. "Hey, Mike, it's all good. I'd be lying in a morgue right now with a tag on my toe if you hadn't been there to keep him busy. I owe you, bro. Big time."

Mike exhaled and clapped a hand over his heart. "Oh, God."

I grinned and lifted another weight onto the opposite side of the bar. Mike and I had only been working together a week, but he was about the most true-blue kid you'd ever want to know. Even though I'd been away from the LGPD a good ten years, I recognized this particular department's fingerprint all over him. This place wasn't just a job. It was a family. Your brothers and sisters had your six no matter what, and it made little difference whether you were on shift or off, whether your call for assistance was for an unruly subject, or a family emergency. ETA, five minutes, armed with either a shotgun or potato salad. I'd forgotten how good it was. Especially the potato salad.

Mike stared blankly into the carpet. "You know, crap like that... Makes you feel stupid lucky, doesn't it?"

I paused and looked at him.

"I mean, what if that day had had our names on it?"

Shaking my head, I replied in a low voice. "It didn't." But my mouth went dry at the words.

"Yeah, but it could of. God, I wouldn't have been around to see my kids grow up."

I pulled a somber grin. His family was still so newly-minted, they sparkled. He never missed a chance to boast about them, or to spin horror stories of the latest child-instigated household disaster.

I sat on the bench press and stared up at him. "How old are they?" I asked.

"Three and nine months," he replied. "I was scared to even tell Nicole what happened," he added, eyebrows raised as if in surprise. I forgot how long they'd been married, but they should have been long past the honeymoon phase. They weren't.

Envy, like an angry dog, snapped at me.

My own reaction surprised me. For the past ten years, coming home to an empty apartment had meant crashing on the couch without taking a shower, twisting open a cold one, and yelling at the game on TV. It was the good life, free of responsibility and differences of opinion. The guys with gold rings on their fingers constantly reminded me how lucky I was, not to mention how smart. I, in turn, extended my condolences for their stupidity.

But I didn't have so much as a gerbil to worry about me while I was on shift.

"Don't let it eat you, Mike," I said—feeling woefully inadequate to offer such advice. "It takes more than that to knock you or me down."

He offered half a smile. "What about you, Mr. Sexiest-Man-Alive? What would you have regretted?"

Fingers splayed, I rubbed my palms together and worked my jaw. What to say? How to control the riot of thoughts screaming through my head, drawing ever nearer a deadly conflict?

I dropped my head into my hands and rubbed my face. "Everything."

Mike chuckled. "Whoa, man."

"No, seriously." I shot him a stern look. "What have I done with my life? Forty-one, and I feel just like I did the day I graduated high school."

"Bet you didn't have gray hair in high school," Mike pointed out.

I mocked a scowl. "Smart-ass. What are you, thirty-two? Thirty-three?"

"Thirty-one."

I hoisted an eyebrow and sighed. "Practically still in rompers."

He snapped me with the towel again.

I laughed and dodged, but my grin faded quickly. Leaning on my knees, I began to count off my observations of his life on my fingers. "You're married."

He smiled. Any mention of Nicole usually made him smile.

"You've got a beautiful family," I continued. His horror stories were always illustrated with snapshots of deceptively adorable children. "You just bought your first house. And everybody agrees you're next in line for a set of stripes on your sleeve. But me? I drift. One place to the next. One department to the next. I throw away good positions because I can't sit still. I don't even know what I'm looking for. Or waiting for."

"We've each got our own path, man."

"Mine staggers like a drunk." I dragged my fingers through my hair, then looked away. Sexiest Man Alive? I told inquiring minds I was merely a confirmed gym rat-slash-health nut. But truth be told, I was burning more than just calories. I was trying to burn away my guilt.

"There's no meaning for me," I said. "What happened the other night—it made me realize; I'm afraid of dying without ever having done anything… anything *real*."

Mike chuckled. "You're a cop, Ryan. It doesn't get any realer than that."

I sighed and didn't answer. I felt like I'd only managed to get my cuffs around one or two of the unruly thoughts rioting in my head. The rest were still surging and screaming. Crushing down on me. Suffocating…

91

What had I accomplished since I'd left my hometown? A twenty-year veteran of law enforcement, and I was working bicycle patrol as a summer reserve officer. My personal life wasn't any shinier. In the ten years since my divorce, I'd simply bounced from one woman to the next— a glorious string of burn-and-die relationships that never amounted to more than a fling. More than one had thought I was there for keeps, but I'd soon set them straight. Broken their hearts. Moved on. Got my tires slashed.

Perhaps the lack of meaning in my life was due to the lack of people in my life who could add meaning to it.

I would have had Monica, if I hadn't thrown her away. But I had. Maybe we would have finally figured out a way to have kids—like Mike's two cubs. Ours would have been older by now, though. Maybe Bailey's age. But of course, Monica and I had wasted money on birth control for years. Turned out, we couldn't have kids anyway. That had been a punch to the gut. Especially for Monica.

In all my wanderings, I'd seen a good chunk of the country and a good chunk of the people in it. But I was alone. At the end of the day, I didn't have anyone to miss me when I was gone. In that light, everything else felt suddenly pointless.

CHAPTER NINETEEN
MONICA

I stormed into the detectives' office and slapped my portfolio down on my desk. What was wrong with me? Why'd I have to go and antagonize Brandt again? Why was it so hard to simply be civil?

"Morning, Monica," Lehman said from the next cubicle over. He leaned back in his office chair to stare at me over the rim of a coffee mug. "I thought you were off still?"

"Shove it up your ass," I snapped, rifling through the notes in my portfolio.

As soon as I'd said it, I pulled up short and rolled my eyes skyward. Damn it. I'd forgotten to be decent yet again. God, I was failing at life.

Screw this.

I dropped into my chair and booted up my computer. "What's happened since I was gone?" I set the yellow legal pad from my portfolio on top of my desk, taking a moment to align the edges of the pad with the laminate corner. Notes on my interview with Bailey Johnson marched across the page in well-ordered bullet points.

"Not much exciting," Lehman said. He eased out of his chair, which groaned from years of misuse and abuse.

Unaccustomed to sitting upright, it slouched permanently into a reclined position, the overstretched springs simply giving up on their strained existence. Lehman sauntered over to my desk and sat on top of the legal pad. I glared at his back-end as it dog-eared the corners of my pages. I nearly opened my mouth to bite his head off, but forced myself to bite my tongue instead. *Be civil, be civil...*

"Hit up Charles Hart's kids and ex-wife," he went on. He stared down at me. "Broke the news to them, of course. Anyway, they all said the same thing. Dear old dad was gay as the day was long, and head-over-heels for his next-door neighbor." He shrugged, his eyes blasé. "Hence the divorce."

Then it was true. Hart had killed Fritz and Jason in a mad bid for Roland's attention. But was that really the end of it? Questions still dogged my thoughts. "Any leads on the accomplice?" I asked.

"Nah. Roland's leads were all junk. Still no sign of the getaway vehicle, either. On the bright side, autopsies are today—both Jason and Charles. When we get the bullets outta them, we'll ship 'em off to the lab. Other than that, we're just waiting to hear on fingerprints from the firearms and the crashed vehicle." He blew across the surface of his coffee and took a sip.

"Well, that accomplice better have left us *something*."

Lehman smirked. "A shit ton of casings. God, they were scattered on the street like acorns under an oak tree."

"Any ID on his weapon?"

He scowled. "Those were .22 LR rimfires, Monica. I crap those after lunch."

I lifted an eyebrow and nodded. So did I. They were cheap as dirt.

"Eh, we'll flush him out. He can't hide forever. So, what are you going to work on today?" he asked.

"Bailey."

"The kid? Didn't you already get her statement?"

"She's gotta remember something about that accomplice."

He gestured with his mug. "Oh, c'mon, Monica. You grilled her for hours Friday night."

"And now that she's had a rest, we can go at it again."

Lehman scowled and lifted his coffee to his mouth with a squint and a tight shake of his head. "If she remembers anything, she'll call you."

I glared at him. "Lehman, somewhere on the face of this earth, there's a man walking loose who played a part in the kidnapping and murder of another human being."

"Well, look at you being so altruistic. He killed a killer," Lehman pointed out. "A *cop* killer. It's weeds choking out weeds, if you ask me. Did us a favor. Jason Thomlin got away scot-free for way too long."

I leaned back and stared at him in disbelief. "Oh, so we're giving this guy a free pass?" I said, turning up a palm. "What if he wasn't just an accomplice? What if he was the mastermind?"

Lehman scowled. "Mastermind? Hart was the one who stood to gain by Fritz and Jason's deaths."

"Was he? Then where did Charles Hart even *find* an accomplice? Who walks into the corner cafe and hits up their coffee buddies with a proposition for murder? 'Hey, Ralph, wanna bump off a couple of dudes with me?'"

"*I* don't know who he hung out with."

I held out an open palm. "Show me Hart's criminal record. Go ahead. Show me. Give me the list of known criminal associates."

Lehman stared at my empty hand, then slurped his coffee loudly. Hart didn't have a record, and he knew it.

I leaned forward and tapped my desk. "There's something more going on. I'm not satisfied with these answers. And I hate Jason Thomlin as much as you do. But I'm not letting his killer get away."

"You know what, Monica? I don't think this has anything to do with the purity of your soul or conspiracy theories or even jackalopes in Easter baskets." He jabbed the mug at me. "You're pissed you didn't spot Charles Hart for a murderer in the first place, and now you're over-compensating."

I ground my teeth and pounded my passcode into my computer. Lehman wasn't doing much to improve my mood.

"Look, don't beat yourself up. Charlie Hart was a lovelorn boyfriend. Any hombre with a broken heart can turn into a killer. We've seen it happen often enough. That's all this case is about."

"You so sure?" I asked.

"The simplest answer is usually the right one."

He shoved off my desk and went back to his own, leaving my legal pad wrinkled and torn. I closed my eyes momentarily, breathed deeply, then meticulously straightened out the pages. Still, I flashed Lehman a scowl before turning to the recording of my interview with Bailey Johnson. I wanted to comb over it again before I called her. Try to find some question I hadn't thought to ask. One sliver of her memory that might lead to an ID of the accomplice.

Chief Erickson strode into the room, glancing over a document in his hand. "Lehman, I was wondering if you could—" He lifted his head and spotted me immediately. "Monica?"

Crap. I ignored him with a vengeance, staring into my computer screen and clutching the mouse in a death grip. He was *not* making me go home.

He snapped his folder shut. "Monica, come into my office."

"Oo," Lehman mock-groaned under his breath.

The tone of the chief's voice reminded me of the time my dad had caught me out after curfew. I'd been making out with Ryan Brandt all night—the saints forgive me for my stupidity.

Fuming, I rose out of my seat. The chief left his document and some brief instructions with Lehman, then led me into his office. He dropped into the chair behind his desk and leaned back, crossing his long legs. "I thought I gave you the day off."

I flicked an eyebrow. "I'm giving it back."

"You won't do this case any good if you're burnt out."

"I'm not burnt out." If only he could have seen me turning my own house upside-down.

"Neumiller and Lehman have been working on it all weekend."

"We'll get this thing solved faster if we all work together."

The chief tilted his white, close-cropped head and studied me with curiosity. "Since when do you 'work together'?"

Well, that stung. I stood a little straighter to show him it didn't.

Wade motioned to one of the chairs in front of his desk. "Sit," he invited.

"No, thank you."

The chief rubbed his temple and shook his head. "Ahhh, Monica," he muttered. "You're lucky I like you." He shot his gaze upward, fixing me icily in the eye. "I said *sit.*"

I felt my chin quiver. I sat.

He smiled. "Good girl."

I hated him.

"Now, what's this all about?"

"It's not 'about' anything. I'm just trying to get my job done." False. Lehman had hit the nail on the head. I was pissed I hadn't recognized Hart as a killer. I was pissed we had no good leads to his accomplice. I was pissed no one saw what I saw in this case. I was equally pissed I couldn't spend five minutes at home without going paranoid over the collapse of my Wall. I needed to be at work. I needed to stay busy. "I've got an instinct about this case, Wade. We're not just looking for a fugitive killer. There's a bigger story here."

He hoisted an eyebrow. "This isn't a complicated case, Monica. A tragic and pointless one, but not complicated."

"Really?" I shot back. "Then what the hell brought Jason and Fritz back to Lake Geneva after all these years?"

Wade shrugged. "Charles lured them somehow."

I gave the chief a scathing look. "Really? We've been looking for seventeen years, for Christ's sake. You're telling me Hart just had their numbers in his contacts?"

He bobbed his head sideways. I'd scored a point. Feeling my victory, I forged on.

"What about the warnings? 'Cleaning house.' Remember? Painted in blood on both Roland and Tommy's windows. If these murders were simply about an over-zealous boyfriend, who left the threats? Who's trying to clean house?"

Wade thought for a moment. "Try this on for size: Jason left the messages. Hart knew Jason had threatened Roland, so he got to Jason first. He didn't have to lure Fritz and Jason back; they came back to kill any leads that might still be strewn around. Hart just saw his opportunity and took it."

"But Charles and Tommy knew nothing. They were cleared of any involvement in the burglary ring."

Wade shrugged. "Paranoia eats you after a while."

I slumped back into my chair. I guess the theory worked. I lifted my hand to my mouth and gnawed violently on my thumbnail.

Wade gave me a pitying look. "You're digging too deep, Monica. It's like I said; not that complicated."

I took my scarred nail out of my mouth. "It's only a theory, what you're proposing," I said.

"Yes, but so is yours—though I'm not quite sure what your theory *is*."

In truth, neither did I. But fear chipped away at me. Fear that we were infinitely behind the game. That we didn't even know what the game *was*. Or when the next round would pop up, pointing a gun between our eyes.

"It'll all come clear, Monica," Wade said. "Just have a little patience."

I ground my teeth against my thumbnail again. "And if somebody else dies?"

"There's no one left to die. Bobby Markham's ring is gone now." He dropped his gaze and fidgeted with his pen. "All three of those boys." I didn't miss the flicker of pain in the chief's eye. Seventeen years ago, he had killed Fritz and Jason's ringleader, Bobby Markham, in a gun fight after their last heist. After all this time, that death still weighed on him. Wade and Bobby's father, Roland Markham, had been childhood friends. There was no getting past something like that.

Wade stirred and grabbed a stack of paperwork. "We'll sort it out once we find that accomplice. Now go home. I don't want to see your face for twenty-four hours."

I sighed "Fine." I got up and strode to the door, but stopped with my hand on the knob, my conversation with Ryan returning to my thoughts. "Wade?" I asked, looking back. "What do you make of that necklace Jason gave to Bailey Johnson?"

He leaned back in his chair and tilted an eyebrow, as if only mildly interested in the topic. "I don't have to theorize about that one. I know."

I snapped to attention. "What do you know?"

Wade slowly twisted his swivel chair. I would have said he looked like an old man sawing away on a rocker on his front porch, staring into the distant past. But he was still too brawny for that metaphor, and he could still kick my ass at the firing range. "It was a gift from Elaina Thomlin to her husband," he said. "For Tommy, when he went into the Navy. Later on, they gave it to Jason."

I contemplated the story in silence. It was weighty with history and meaning. "Why would he give it to Bailey?"

Wade shrugged. "Maybe he thought she could bring it back to his dad. An heirloom like that doesn't belong in the streets, or worse yet, in a cardboard box at the morgue."

"He told her to keep it."

Wade shook his head. "I don't know, Monica. Maybe he was just delirious."

I looked down and fidgeted with the door knob. "Brandt thinks I should give it back."

"I'm surprised you kept it."

"I don't have any answers on it yet."

"If he'd kept it around his neck instead of giving it to Bailey, you wouldn't have thought twice about it." Wade screwed up his face and shook his head. "Give it back to her, Monica. Or I can hand it to Tommy, and he can decide what to do with it."

I nodded, reluctantly. I couldn't stand an unanswered question. But the chief was right. "I'll put in a call to the DA and the ME. If they're okay with it, I'll go bust it out of evidence."

"Good. And *then...?*" He left off with a leading question.

I glared at him out of the corner of my eye. "And then I'll go home."

He nodded deeply, but refrained from saying *good girl* again.

I left his office and made for the elevator. I would obey orders—but only because it was clear I couldn't hide in a building this small. That didn't mean I was going to quit working on the case, though. A jog around the lake ought to clear my mind and shake some ideas loose. It had been a good year since I'd run the entire Lake Shore Path—a twenty-one mile circuit. Legend had it, two boys had run around the lake twice in a single day back in the '70s, and even stopped for a swim. I'd always had an itch to challenge that record. Or if that wouldn't do, maybe I could clean out the attic. Finish the entire basement. Turn the damn house upside down and balance it on the chimney, just for shits and giggles.

Anything but stop and think.

When the elevator let me out, I made for the evidence intake room. If this long chain of custody were true, then the necklace now belonged legally to Bailey—even though, like the rest of the world, this state of affairs didn't make a damn bit of sense.

CHAPTER TWENTY
RYAN

I grit my teeth. Grunted. Strained for just one more rep. The bruises across my pecs and abs made me all too aware of their presence as they yelled in agony. Quite possibly, today was not the day to aim for max reps of my own body weight on the bench press. The first five or six hadn't felt so bad. By ten, I was hurting. By twelve, I was just an idiot. Worse yet, Schultz had left, and I didn't have a spotter to grab the bar in case my arms gave out. What had I been thinking?

As usual, I hadn't been thinking at all.

Giving it everything I had, I finally locked out my elbows and threw the weights into the brackets with a clatter. I cussed and let my arms flop to my sides like broken wings.

"Hell, you look like crap."

I turned my head. The man who stood there didn't look as if he ever darkened the door of a gym. Sixty-something and white-haired, his pot belly pulled against his black shirt, and the distinctive white patch of his clerical collar was nearly eclipsed by his round, flushed face.

I sat up, swung my feet to the floor, and swatted the vinyl-covered bench. "Take your place, donut."

"Keep your guts and brawn. I'll stick to fighting the devil." Chaplain Bill Gallagher grinned and shook his head. "So the prodigal really has come home." He spread his arms. "Come here, you runt."

I stood up and wiped the sweat off my face and chest with a towel. "I stink."

He corralled me into an embrace and thumped my back, leaving me no choice but to hug him in return.

"Where you been, old man?" I asked, shaking his hand between us in a firm grip. "You missed all the action."

"Visiting the in-laws. Both of 'em in their nineties, and still living at home."

"Wow. Good on them."

"No in-law should live as long as they have. Payment for my sins, I reckon." He rocked his head back and guffawed, then slapped me on the shoulder. "Sit your arse down, kid, and catch me up."

I grinned as I took my seat on the bench press again. He pulled up a chair opposite me. As I looked into Bill Gallagher's smiling eyes, I finally realized it might actually be good to be home.

"You heard about the homicides?" I asked.

"Hell, I heard all about those in the hallway. Tell me about you."

I shifted uncomfortably. It was easier to talk about work. I gave him a stunted run-down of my activities since I'd left Lake Geneva ten years ago—all the departments I'd worked in. All the positions I'd held. I tried to make it sound glowing—one adventure after another.

He scowled at me. "What kind of an idiot gives up a sergeant's salary in Minneapolis for a temp job pedaling a bicycle in a tourist town?"

I felt my face redden and dropped my gaze to my hands. Bill was never afraid to call bullshit. I shrugged. "Same idiot who gives up a detective's badge in Madison for a patrol car in Grand Rapids. I don't like it when things stay the same, I guess."

"The pay, man, the pay! Benefits? Pension? Retirement? Ever think about that?"

My muscles tensed. "Sure, I do."

"You just don't care."

"I care."

"You're scared."

"What?"

"You're scared a sumthin'."

"Like what?"

"Responsibility."

I scowled at him. "Nice try, Freud. I would have ditched the badge years ago if I was afraid of responsibility."

"Personal commitments."

I opened my mouth, but nothing came out.

"Ah!" He smiled and pointed a finger. "Shot in the dark, but not bad, if I do say so myself. You didn't know Monica was working here again, did you?"

I closed my mouth and shook my head.

"I thought a callin' you to warn ya, but it sounded like more fun this way."

I raised an eyebrow at him. "Thanks."

"What're pals for?"

The door swung open. Bill and I both looked up. To my surprise, Monica herself stood there. She glanced between the two of us. Great. Just what I needed—for Monica to catch me in the middle of a heart-to-heart with the chaplain. I braced myself for a snarky remark.

But she kept her tongue between her teeth. "Here," was all she said. She tossed a plastic bag across the room.

I caught it. It was an evidence bag. Inside was a tiny metal ship's wheel on a ball chain. A piece of paper stapled to the closure listed the chain of custody—me, then Monica, then the evidence room, then Monica again. It was a photocopy. The original would be carefully filed away. The

final line on the form bore the notation, *Released to Off.*
Ryan Brandt to be returned to owner, and was signed and
dated.

By the time I'd looked up to thank her, she was gone.

"Woman of few words," Bill observed, "unless you get
her riled." He chortled, then stood up, slapping his thighs.
"Well, Ryan, if you ever need help..." He walked to the door,
then stopped and grinned back at me. "You know where the
state mental hospital is."

"How does an ass like you keep a job like this?" I asked.

He jabbed a thumb upwards. "I pay off the higher-ups."
He winked and pulled open the door. "See ya 'round, kid."

I fingered the little charm through the plastic and
thought of Bailey. The truth was, I *was* floundering—worse
now than before. I'd somehow believed everything would
come clear just by coming home. But it was exactly the
opposite. I'd never felt as mired-down as I did now.

"Bill?"

He stopped. "Yeah?"

I turned the plastic bag around in my hands.
Procrastinating. When it came right down to it, it was hard
to force the words out of my mouth.

"Yeah," I finally admitted. "I could use some help."

CHAPTER TWENTY-ONE
JIMMY

Three padlocks and a deadbolt later, Jimmy swung open the door to his secret lab with a flourish. He watched Markham duck through the low entry, hands tucked inside his cardigan pockets.

"Well, well, well," the old man said, glancing around. "You've been very busy in here."

Jimmy sauntered in and allowed himself a smug expression. "It's nothing, really." And it wasn't, in all honestly. It was, or used to be, a backyard shed. In one corner, a stack of garden tools and bags of mulch hailed back to the structure's former purpose. But the rest of the shack had succumbed to progress and the scientific method.

An extensive chemistry set took up the workbench on one whole wall. The shelves in back were stuffed with carefully-labeled jars and crates full of electrical components and building materials—wood and scrap metal and plastic—for designing experiments. One corner of the shed housed his computer, perched on a rusted iron table that had originally displayed a flower pot. The third wall was covered in drifts of paper, secured to the rough-finished boards by thumbtacks. The sheets were crammed with charts, diagrams, and equations. A drawing table underneath it was nearly lost in mounds of drafting paper, pens, and rulers. A scientific calculator currently served as a paperweight. Jimmy's entire paycheck went toward scientific equipment.

Markham leaned forward to study the diagrams on the wall: electromagnetic force, light waves, the odd subatomic particle. "You drew these?" he asked.

Jimmy pushed his glasses up his nose and hooked his thumbs through his belt loops. "Yep."

He pointed to one. "What is this?"

"Wardenclyffe Tower. Nikola Tesla started building it in 1901, but never finished. It was supposed to provide wireless electricity to the whole world."

"Never finished?"

"Yeah. His backer pulled out when he realized there was no way to put a meter on it and charge for the electricity being used. No one's been able to reproduce Tesla's idea—at least not on the same scale." He rocked on his heels. "I've toyed with the design."

"Fascinating," the old man murmured, shaking his head. "Have you produced a prototype?"

"Nah," Jimmy replied. "Not one that works."

"Well, I'm sure you'll figure it out," Markham replied. "Something like this would revolutionize modern life, every bit as much as the Internet and the smartphone. Imagine the implications for electric cars. You could drive forever, so long as you had coverage."

Jimmy eyed his diagram critically. He hadn't thought of electric cars. He was just sick of going to recharge his phone, only to realize he'd lost his charger. Again.

"And this?" Markham pointed to another drawing. It resembled a submarine, but with a rigid box tail fin instead of adjustable diving planes.

"That's Little Boy," Jimmy said, "the first atomic bomb ever used in war." Conveniently parked near the diagram, on top of Jimmy's drafting table, was a 1:200-scale model of a Boeing B-29 Superfortress bomber, the name *Enola Gay* inscribed under the cockpit. "That's the plane that dropped the bomb."

Markham tilted his head back to study the drawing through his spectacles. "Hiroshima," he said reverently.

"Yeah." Jimmy nodded. "That one was nothing." He pointed to another diagram. "This was Tsar Bomba—the king of bombs. The Russians set it off north of the Arctic Circle in 1961. It was the arms race, you know. They were testing the newest munitions."

The old man nodded. "Yes, I remember those days."

"This baby was hundreds of times more powerful than the bombs they used in Japan," Jimmy said. "It set off shock waves that were detected around the entire world—*three separate times.* It nearly killed the plane crew who dropped it."

Markham's eyes drifted over maps and photos of Hiroshima and Nagasaki. Jimmy never tired of those images—cities flattened. In some places, nothing but a shadow remained where a human being had stood the moment before.

"Such unspeakable power," Markham muttered. He shook his head. "Such loss of life."

Jimmy pushed his hands into his pockets. "Yeah," he said under his breath. "Pretty sweet."

Markham raised an eyebrow at him. He hitched up his trouser legs and slid onto the tall stool in front of Jimmy's drawing board. "This, Jimmy." He waved his hand toward the diagrams. "This is not the road for you."

Jimmy's mouth dropped open. He gaped a moment, then shook his head. "You're wrong. This is the *only* road for me. I've already dedicated years of my life to the study of explosives engineering. You're telling me I'm supposed to throw all that away? Not to mention the sense of euphoria my work applies to my neurological condition."

The old man's body heaved as he chuckled. "That's not really what I meant. We all have our passions in life, and we must follow them. Otherwise, we're only ever empty shells of our true selves. No, I have no doubt you will master the field of explosives engineering. But how will you put it to use, young man? By blowing up an abandoned barn? Taking out a pier and a pair of boats that are very much in use? What will that get you in the end?"

Jimmy stared at him a moment or two, blinking.

"Juvenile hall, Jimmy," said the old man flatly, "juvenile hall. It's very hard to win a Nobel from inside a detention facility."

Jimmy closed his mouth and nodded.

Markham eyed the diagrams and photographs again. "Sadly, I doubt we'll ever see the day when there is no need for these monstrous creations. As long as one exists, there must be a dozen more, stronger still, to keep it in check. And where there are bombs, there must be people who study them—not to take lives, but to save them, to find ways to counteract their devastation." He nodded. "Yes, I fear there may be need of your skill yet. But tell me, Jimmy. These bombs. Why are they so important to you?"

"They fascinate me."

"Why?"

Jimmy shut his mouth and swallowed. He'd never really stopped to ask, but he knew the answer anyway. It would be supremely satisfying to witness millions of people obliterated. Cities shaken to the ground. Miles of earth rendered desolate, radioactive wasteland. All because he sketched a diagram. He couldn't even say how much he wanted to control that kind of power, merely by pushing a pencil from the comfort of his drawing board. But the old man was waiting for an answer.

"I'd blow up the whole solar system, if I could," he finally said. Perhaps hyperbole would get him past the uncomfortable question of why he felt the urge to kill.

Instead of appearing shocked, the old man looked deeper into Jimmy's eyes. "You would exterminate life altogether? Yourself included? What would you gain?"

"What would anyone lose?" Jimmy shot back. "We spin on our axis and fly in circles around the sun. Millions of life forms have existed before us. They've all exhausted their brief, meaningless time spans and fought for every minute of it. There are more species that have gone extinct than are alive on the planet today. They all die. What's the point? Why *not* end it all?"

Markham nodded somberly. "You make a valid argument. Particularly if you discount the fleeting beauties that our existence has to offer. Love. Happiness. Peace. These are, ultimately, why we struggle for those hard-earned minutes of our lives. A man will endure excruciating pain for fifty-nine minutes out of the sixty, if the sixtieth will bring him joy."

Jimmy felt his face flush red-hot. He tried to tell himself that this concept of *love* was nothing; a release of chemicals into the bloodstream. It wasn't necessary to survival. But at the same time, at the mere mention of the word, he wanted to cry, and then he wanted to ransack his own lab, and then he wanted to stab the old man with broken shards from his chemistry set. Had he ever been loved? No. Not long enough to matter.

Jimmy pushed the thoughts away and straightened his spine. "My bombs bring me joy."

"A metal shell full of unstable material? They take no joy in *you*. They can't love you back. Surely there's someone in the world you love, Jimmy."

A face flashed before Jimmy's memory, so unexpected it caused a temporary neural imbalance. He thought he'd all but forgotten that face, so tiny and trusting and admiring to a fault.

"My big brother's the smartest kid in school." Her voice echoed through his head as if in an empty lecture hall. *"Maybe even the world!"*

Granted, you don't love a sister the way you crush over a cute girl in study hall. But what he'd once felt for his little sister... The way he'd let her follow him around. Taught her everything he knew. Love was the only word for it.

Markham's question hung in the air, waiting for an answer. Jimmy made up his mind. The crush, he could talk about. But his sister lived in a part of his soul where he didn't venture anymore. The door was marked with every hazard warning known to science.

He would talk about Bailey instead.

He sighed and pulled back the diagram of Tsar Bomba. Beneath was a diagram unlike any of the others. There were no labels with arrows pointing to the various parts. There were no notations on size, distance, quantity, or materials. There were no formulas, no equations.

It was a sketch of Bailey Johnson. Not one of his best. How do you draw a curve of hair you can't precisely measure? How do you triangulate the distance between eyes, nose, and mouth? How do you quantify the soul, as it sparkles in the eyes?

"Who is this?" Markham asked.

"Her name is Bailey. Bailey Johnson. We're in the same grade, and we work together."

"Oh, your girlfriend?"

Jimmy shook his head. "She won't go out with me. I've shown her the statistical likelihood of a good match—when 'good' is defined as the greatest possible level of enjoyment combined with the longest possible timespan of our relationship, but she just—"

Markham shook his head. "No, Jimmy. You're thinking with this." He tapped his temple. "That won't get you anywhere. You need to think with *this*."

He reached forward and touched Jimmy lightly on the chest. Jimmy felt his heart flutter in response, as if rebooted by a defibrillator. In truth, Jimmy had forgotten that particular organ was there, beyond, of course, its basic functions of circulating blood. For the first time in years, he felt something that could only be defined as hope. Possibility.

The sensation was mildly disturbing. Not because it was particularly unpleasant. It wasn't. But he couldn't measure or define it. Truth be told, it frightened him. And yet, the sensation was addictively appealing, like a chemical substance that created a physical dependency after the very first use.

Still, he didn't understand it. He rubbed hard behind his ear and looked intently at the old man. "But... how does one think with one's heart?"

"Well, you *might* start," he replied, "by rephrasing the question with the use of personal pronouns."

"Personal pronouns?"

Markham nodded slowly, encouragingly, like a teacher awaiting the pupil's answer.

Jimmy thought hard and finally asked, timidly, as if the words were covered with rust, "How... do I think... with my heart?"

Markham grinned broadly. "There now. That's more like it."

CHAPTER TWENTY-TWO
RYAN

With the necklace in my jeans pocket, I walked through the door of the Geneva Bar and Grill and breathed the scent of steak and fries. The well-worn path through the paint on the cement floor suggested the food tasted as good as it smelled. Despite that stirring testimony, I couldn't help my suspicions that the aroma of down-home cooking merely masked the rot that hid underneath. Hanging near the door to the dining room was a weathered life ring painted with the letters *S.O.S.* Fitting, somehow.

The front counter was decorated with hemp rope and metal lanterns with red and green glass for port and starboard, but the counter itself was abandoned. I peered into the dining room and scanned the crowd.

Like a bomb dog to explosives, my eye went immediately to Bud Weber, the owner. His meaty hands grasped four pitchers, two apiece, each foaming with beer. He set them down in the middle of a long table, all the while grinning and exchanging banter with his guests. I recognized one or two of them as his cronies from the last time I'd dropped by, but others were new faces to me. I found myself taking note of their physical features, hair styles, clothing, piercings, tattoos. I didn't trust Weber, and I wanted to know at a glance if I ever crossed paths with one of his crew.

Weber leaned over a young woman to drop off the last pitcher. In what was perhaps the worst bit of acting I'd ever seen, he pretended to trip on a chair leg and nearly pour the beer down the young lady's low-cut tee shirt. He "saved" himself just in time—but only after he'd had a good peek. He guffawed. She pretended to be offended, but laughed with the rest of the table, even as the dirty jokes went around at her expense.

She couldn't have been older than twenty-one, barely old enough to drink. Way too young for the likes of Weber. I felt the heat rise under my collar. I'd never rest until I found a way to get Bailey away from him.

He must have felt my eyes on him. He glanced up and did a double take. He probably hadn't recognized me immediately, out of uniform. But the look in his eyes when it finally clicked clearly indicated discomfort. They darted to the young woman and back, as if he were wondering how much I'd seen. I kept a straight face and a slightly hardened stare. *Plenty, buddy. I saw plenty.*

Hypocrite, a voice nagged in the back of my head.

I tried to stuff it down, but it wouldn't go. My conscience was being straight with me, and I hated it. I was pretty sure I'd played that same prank myself in the not-too-distant past. Seen my pals pull similar stunts. I'd laughed back then. I'd spent nights with women half my age.

Somehow, it was different when the man in question was supposed to be the father of a teenage girl—even if only a temporary one. I shook my head to clear my mind. Bizarre how Bailey had forced me to see so many things differently. It was as if she'd put my world on a tilt and given it a firm swat to shake loose everything that didn't need to stick.

Weber excused himself from the group and made his way over to me. "Hey, there. Ryan, isn't it? How's it goin'?"

I skipped the pleasantries. "Is Bailey here?"

My brusque reply gave him pause. He shifted his weight back slightly. "Yeah, she's here. Somethin' wrong?"

I thought about Bailey's bruises and wanted to dish up a piece of my mind for him, but held back. The best way to get a confession was to keep it cool between us. Convince him I was no threat. Maybe even build some rapport, if I could stomach it.

I hated kissing his ass.

"I just have something to give her," I said.

"Sure thing. I'll send her out."

"How's she doing?" I asked.

He froze mid-step with a look on his face like whirring gears. I'd left the question ambiguous on purpose. A guilty man might be thinking about the last time he took a belt to his victim. An innocent man—a man who cared about the child under his guardianship—would think immediately about the fact that the girl had just witnessed a double homicide.

I didn't like Weber's long pause.

"She's fine," he said at last. But his eyes still suggested he hadn't caught up with the conversation.

"I'm sure she told you," I said, still keeping it vague.

The light finally flickered on. He closed his mouth, which had been hanging open, and wiped a hand across his five-o'clock shadow. "Oh, gee, yeah. Yeah, we talked about it." He shook his head. "Can't believe somethin' like that happening to my Bailey. The killing and all? Wow. She's fine, though. She's a tough kid."

"Yes, she is." It was perhaps the only thing we could agree on. That girl was made of iron. Unfortunately, the iron took the shape of a fortified bunker between her and the world.

"She says you took real good care of her—you know, through the interrogation, and all," he added. "Said it was real comforting having you around, after all that crap."

What a lie. Bailey barely tolerated my presence, and I knew it. Weber was only looking to butter me up. I couldn't have been more disgusted if he'd literally smeared bacon fat over my body. I told myself to accept the compliment— all part of whittling him down to that eventual confession—but somehow, I just couldn't get a *thank you* past the hard stare that had frozen across my face.

He motioned over his shoulder. "I guess I'll go get her for you."

I nodded. He lumbered through a doorway to the kitchen and left me standing in the front room.

I reached into my pocket and fingered the plastic bag containing the necklace. I wondered once again about its true meaning. Why Jason Thomlin had given it to her. Why she'd wanted to keep it. Maybe one day, she'd trust me with the answers.

Bill Gallagher and I had had a long conversation. I'd told him everything. The anxiety over Bailey and her probable abuse. The daily strain from rubbing shoulders with Monica, and the guilt I felt for how I'd treated her. The sense that nothing I'd done in my life really mattered—that to the contrary, I'd only ever left misery in my wake.

It was my fault Monica was such a viper nowadays. Granted, she'd always been bad-ass. But she also used to have a beautiful smile. The mere memory of it warmed my heart. I was the reason that smile had died. I'd hoped that in the ten years we'd been apart, it would have had a chance to flicker back to life. Clearly not. I'd snuffed it out permanently. I felt the loss keenly.

It was also my fault Bailey was in foster care. I doubted she remembered the role I'd played in her life—that I was the one who'd found her cowering in a closet in her mother's boyfriend's house. She'd been so young, only five.

And I would have been only one of many strangers in uniform she'd seen that night—buried in full tactical gear, probably looking more like a phenomenon from a military sci-fi movie than a human being.

I'd all but forgotten her myself, until I'd seen those big, round eyes, staring out at the world without the slightest hint of emotion. They hadn't changed, and they'd sucked me back in time to that first night. It was true, there was nothing I could have done differently, as Bill was quick to point out. I'd followed protocol. I'd worked with the systems we had in place for such situations. But I couldn't put it out of my mind that I was the one who had taken her from her mother and turned her over to the state. I'd thought at the time I was saving her. Little could I have guessed she would still be a ward of the county today, a lifetime later, and that her situation wasn't any better.

"Don't carry more weight than what's your due," Bill had advised me. "Otherwise, you'll turn out like me." He'd slapped his spare tire and laughed.

After my talk with the chaplain, I'd taken the liberty of running a background check on Bud Weber. His history was so clean, the shine of it hurt my eyes. Barely more than a parking ticket. On paper, he looked like a saint. Business owner. Chamber of Commerce member. Even a foster caregiver. I wouldn't have been surprised if his office was plastered with awards for outstanding service to his community. The guy donated trees to the city parks, for Christ's sake.

A tiny teenage girl emerged from the kitchen. She approached me timidly, her hands in the pockets of a small black apron, her eyes wary.

"Hey, Bailey." I gave her a smile, which wasn't returned. "I dropped by your house, but no one was home. Figured you must be here."

She said nothing, as usual. I wondered how she ever took the customers' orders.

117

Clearing my throat, I pulled the plastic bag out of my pocket. I ripped open the heat seal across the top and poured the necklace out into my palm, then carefully found the ends and lifted it up for Bailey to see.

She merely stared.

"I guess we're done with it now," I said. "You can have it back."

She finally pulled one hand out of her apron pocket and held her palm open. I lowered the charm into her hand. She stared down at it.

"I talked with our chaplain today," I told her. She didn't have to know we'd mostly talked about me. "He said he'd give you a call. Did he?"

She nodded.

My chest filled with hope. "Did you have a good talk?"

"He left me a message," she said.

In other words, she'd let it go to voice mail, and hadn't bothered to call back.

"You should set up a time with him," I said. "He's really great."

She nodded noncommittally.

I filled my lungs and glanced around for Weber. He wasn't within sight. I lowered my voice. "Bailey, you can talk to any one of us. Anytime. You've got my number. You can call me whenever you need to. On duty, off duty, day, night—I don't care. Okay?"

She nodded.

I tried my hardest to catch her eye. "Especially if you're scared," I said. "If you're hurting. I want to hear from you."

Her jaw tightened.

"I just... I want you to be happy," I finished.

She quirked a smile, as if I'd made a pathetic joke. Her eyes remained dead. It was one of the most heartbreaking things I'd ever seen.

I didn't want to leave her. But there was no point in carrying on a one-sided conversation all night when she was supposed to be working. I didn't want to get her in trouble with Weber. Besides, I had an early shift the next morning. I was becoming less of a bicycle patrol officer and more of a "wherever-we-need-you" officer. Either they wanted a man of my experience to fill in for regular patrol duty, or I really sucked at riding a bike.

I wanted to give Bailey a comforting touch on the shoulder but knew it wouldn't be received well. "You take care, Bailey," I said instead. "I'll see you soon."

She didn't so much as nod. So I turned and pushed through the door to the parking lot.

If there was a way through her iron barricade, I didn't have a clue how to find it. Maybe that door had fused shut ages ago.

CHAPTER TWENTY-THREE
BAILEY

As the cop walked away, I stared down at the silver wheel in my hand. I'd thought I wanted it back, but now I had it, all the crappy memories of that night—the night of the killing—flashed back into my head like a train wreck. The little bright pops of light. The windshield cracking, spiderweb-style. Somebody screaming. Sharp bits of asphalt grinding into my knees as I leaned over the man with the wavy hair and watched him die. I squeezed my fist around the ship's wheel and fought against the tears pricking the corners of my eyes.

I'd promised the man with the wavy hair that I'd keep the charm. Why had I said that? Why had it even been such a big deal to him? He'd been dying at the time, breathing through holes in his chest while he bled through his nose and mouth. He must have been out of his mind. I probably would have been.

A bulky shadow lowered over me. I whirled and stared up at Bud, my mouth gaping.

"You gonna take these to your table or what?" he asked, holding a pair of plates piled with steak and potatoes. Brown gravy dripped over the edge and ran across his fingers. If it burned, he didn't flinch. The gravy hit the floor with a smack.

I shoved the necklace into my apron pocket and took the plates. "Yes, sir."

He scowled after me as I scurried into the dining room, heart pounding. If I called Ryan every time I was scared, he'd soon get sick of hearing from me.

Forcing a smile, I delivered the plates to a pair of men in yellow safety vests and dirt-caked boots. "Medium rare?" I asked.

One of them raised his hand. I set down the plates one after another—

And suddenly found my eyes transfixed to a nail head in the rough-hewn tabletop, just off the tip of Medium Rare's steak knife. This was *the* table. The one *he* had sat at—the man with the wavy hair. I could visualize the exact spot where the coffee mug had sat, and under it, the hundred-dollar tip. If he'd never left that tip, I never would have chased him out into the parking lot. Never would have seen him kidnapped. Never would have followed him...

"Missy?"

The construction worker's harsh tone snapped my eyes away from the nail head. The scowl on his face suggested he'd been trying to get my attention for some time.

"Tabasco?" he said, waving a fork impatiently.

I pulled a bottle out of my apron and thunked it down where the hundred dollar bill had been, hoping the hot sauce might burn away the memory. Instead, the silver ship's wheel burned in my pocket.

"Anything else?" I whispered, my voice suddenly all dry like sand.

"Nah."

I turned and hurried to the back room. The dish washing machine churned violently, but Jimmy was nowhere to be seen. Maybe he was in the kitchen. His fifty-gallon trash can reeked of every dish in the house, making my stomach roil worse than before.

I could never wear the necklace. Why the hell was I supposed to keep it? Why had I promised? Why had I ever asked to have it back from the police? I pulled it out of my pocket and stared at it. It twinkled at me innocently, reflecting the fluorescent lights off the tips of its tiny spokes, but triggering a burst of fury and anger and terror that tore at me like a garbage disposal.

My gaze flickered between the necklace and Jimmy's trash can.

WEDNESDAY
JUNE 25, 2014

CHAPTER TWENTY-FOUR
BUD

Standing under a tree, Bud eyed the Riviera from a cool distance. The little brick building stood all grand and pretentious, like so many of the buildings around the lake—arches and square corner towers and shit, with morning sunshine sparkling off the windows. He drew deeply on a cigarette. The first rays of daylight brightened the smoke as it poured out of his nose, all white and heavenly like a cherub's ass-cushion.

Mornings were fantastic. After all, getting up with the birds was one of the seven deadly habits of highly effective people. And Bud meant to be highly effective this morning.

Normally, he'd be firing up the grills at the bar. Right now, however, they were sitting cold. Hunks of marbled beef huddled in trays in the walk-in cooler, waiting to be thrown into the oven with spuds and baby carrots and his mom's secret spice mix. No matter. A dead cow could wait. His task couldn't. Not anymore. Not with that nosy cop still poking around, asking about Bailey.

He let the nicotine fill his lungs and calm him down. Released the smoke slowly through his nose. He was just a pedestrian. Just standing in the park, pretending to enjoy the morning and the view. No reason to be furtive about it. Tommy Thomlin didn't know what he looked like, and that was an advantage. But Bud knew what Tommy looked like by now.

His target had been easy to identify: An old man who showed up bright and early every morning, an army-issue haversack slung over his shoulder and a stack of newspapers under one arm. He would walk under the archways and straight to the Mailboat.

It had to be the captain.

Bud had been watching the old man for nearly a week now, ever since that cop had first come a-calling. Bud snorted and knocked the ashes off his cig. What he did with his kid was nobody's business but his own.

Bud, of course, had denied everything. And Bailey had kept her mouth shut. Too afraid of another *ron-day-voo* with his leather belt, no doubt. He grinned. She was a good girl.

But he didn't need cops buzzing around, especially now. He was in too much trouble on too many fronts. He needed to make sure no one raised a ruckus about Bailey again, or the whole kit-and-caboodle might come apart.

Worse, he needed to make sure he didn't lose her.

The thought sent a cold chill down his spine and churned the steak, eggs, and bacon he'd had for breakfast. He'd invested too much time in Bailey, grooming her to his tastes. From the start, she had bent to his will, the way a spaghetti noodle curls around a fork. She was perfect. An angel. A dream.

Clearly, other dudes who signed up for the foster care program were cut from a different cloth than he was, and maybe that was a good thing for the moral fiber of America. Bud hadn't found it so hard to sneak into their ranks. The system was freakin' desperate for homes, and Jesus lovin' Christ, they even paid you for the privilege. Imagine that!

As soon as he'd found out single guys could be foster parents, he'd signed right up.

Surprisingly, Bud looked pretty damn good on paper. Even passed a background check. After all, you only got a police record if you'd been caught. The poor paper pushers over at social services had no idea. As for personality, he should have won an Oscar for the act he put on every time the social workers came around. Even the damn cop had walked away empty-handed.

Bud filled his lungs again and pushed out a stream of smoke. So what if he had kinky desires? That was nobody's business but his. Nobody wanted the kid anyway.

But the boat captain was another thing. He was a troublemaker. It was the captain who had reported Bailey's bruises in the first place and brought the cops down on him. Time to make sure that never happened again. He had a certain point to make to the old man, and he meant for that point to come across loud and clear.

So he watched. Sometimes from behind a tree or a building. Sometimes just standing in plain sight, like he was today. He was making notes. His subject's activities. Schedule. Habits.

On Thursday and Friday last week, the old man had shown up ten minutes before the hour, on the dot. Bud wasn't sure about Saturday; he'd been too busy dumping his car and getting stone drunk. Sunday through Tuesday had proved interesting. The captain was arriving progressively earlier every day, which was extremely useful. He was alone. The shoreline was abandoned. His mail jumpers wouldn't show up for a while yet—not even Bailey, who was also ten minutes early every morning. Funny. She was never that punctual about getting to the bar. He'd have to have a talk with her. He didn't like this other guy getting preferential treatment.

Bud straightened as he caught a glimpse of an old man carrying a tan haversack over his shoulder. Bud took his cigarette out of his mouth and checked his watch. Full twenty minutes before the hour. He grinned. Twenty minutes was more than enough time to play with. He should act now before the subject changed his routine. He glanced around. The grassy park on the brink of the lake was empty. So was the street. It was too freakin' early for the tourists to be out, and the shops and restaurants were still closed. He stomped out his cigarette and hitched his jeans. The adrenaline started to flow, accompanied by whatever that other crap is that makes you feel happy.

Just as he started forward, a breeze passed his shoulder and a jogger whipped by, her blond ponytail bouncing against her back. She ran straight toward the Riviera. Bud cussed—and cussed again when she stopped at the fountain in front of the Riv. She stretched her calves, bracing one tennie on the lip of the basin, then the other. Bud waited. She pulled out her phone. Sat down. Thumbed her screen.

Bud drummed his fingers on his hips. That damned health nut was in no hurry to shove off. He waited. Struck up a new light and waited a full five minutes. Ten. Time was wasting while that little bitch shared kitten videos on Facebook. Meanwhile, the captain's shadow moved around inside the boat, just beyond his reach.

A small dash of color bobbed down the street from the opposite direction. Bailey, dressed in denim shorts and a red long-sleeved tee shirt. Bud cussed and slinked backward down the sidewalk, hoping Bailey didn't see him. That was the nail in the coffin. His chance was gone.

He turned and stomped off, flinging his cig down on the street. Well, the old man had gotten off this time. Not for long, though. Bud would be back.

CHAPTER TWENTY-FIVE
BAILEY

My footsteps drummed down the pier toward the Mailboat. I poked a finger into the pocket of my shorts and touched the necklace again. In the end, I'd saved it from the fate of Jimmy's garbage can. But I'd had it for three days now and never worn it. Instead, I kept it in my pocket every day and under my pillow at night.

I stirred the tiny balls of the silver chain until I felt the little knobby spokes of the ship's wheel. The guy with the wavy hair had been so nice to me when I waited his table. Asked all the questions adults did when they met you for the first time and were thinking about adopting you—but pretending they weren't, because nothing was for sure in foster care. *Where do you go to school? What do you want to study in college? What do you want to be when you grow up?*

Why had he asked all those questions? Why had he given me the necklace? And for the love of God, why had he died? Why hadn't the cosmos given him even half a chance to follow through on all those hinted promises? I pushed back against the tears and snapped my finger out of my pocket. My head felt all twisted up inside.

I stepped through the door into the Mailboat and found Tommy opening the hatch in the middle of the deck, getting ready to climb down the stubby little ladder to the cramped engine compartment. I took a good, hard look at him—you know, while trying not to look like I was looking. I hoped the funky mood that had been following him around might be gone.

"Morning, Tommy," I tried tentatively, twisting a strap that dangled from my backpack.

He glanced up. "Morning." He grinned broadly, but the smile was pasted-on; and while he made sure to meet my eye, his own were dead and colorless.

I twisted the webbing harder. For maybe the first time in my life, I decided to take the bold approach. "You okay?" All right, maybe not *that* bold. But my heart was beating out of my chest. I wasn't good at asking people questions, or at conversation in general.

"Oh yeah," he said dismissively, and his voice would have sounded all chipper and normal if it hadn't been so forced. He grabbed his engine checklist off the edge of the deck and disappeared into the compartment below. This conversation was clearly over.

Yeah, something was totally wrong. And anything that flattened Tommy out like roadkill had to be pretty major.

I dumped my backpack in a chair, pulled a spray bottle and paper towels out of the cupboard, and started spritzing down windows. Whatever was bothering Tommy, it really wasn't my business. He never talked about personal stuff. Not that I never wondered. Sometimes I pictured what his family might be like—a wife, a bunch of kids, an army of grandchildren. From the simple gold ring on his left hand, I'd materialized a dozen faces I'd never met. They were the luckiest people alive, and I was jealous. But what right did an outsider like me have to want in? So I merely pressed my nose against the glass, like a snow-bitten street urchin looking into a bright, warm toy store, longing for everything I couldn't have.

I still wanted to tell him about the shooting. What I'd seen. Maybe even what I'd done. How I'd cried over a dead man I'd never known, but had somehow felt connected to. Maybe Tommy could help me make sense of it all, like he always did.

But now there was something so weird in the air, I didn't dare open my mouth. Partly because Tommy was clearly in his own world right now, and partly because I was beginning to realize that the moment I said, "I saw a guy get killed the other night," I was going to break down and bawl like a two-year-old. And maybe it would become all too obvious how much I just wanted Tommy to pull me into a hug—to shatter the window and haul me in to where it was safe and warm. And maybe he simply wouldn't. He'd just stand there and look awkward while I cried my eyes out because he didn't actually *want* to let me in. And then I'd just want to kill myself.

I choked back my tears, shot a blast of lemon-scented cleaner at the window, and rubbed away a tiny bouquet of nose prints, down low by the sill. The pair of hand prints next to it were so small... I wiped them into oblivion, my heart breaking inside and falling down like little shattered raindrops.

Noah, the other jumper, stepped onto the boat five minutes late, as usual. His tee shirt was only half tucked into his shorts. If it had been possible to wear a shirt sideways, I'm sure he would have tried it just for laughs. His blond bangs hung in his eyes in a way that made some of the girls at school swoon. But most just rolled their eyes and called him a goof.

He swung his backpack into a chair. A pencil dropped out of an unclosed zipper and a tattered notebook poked out. The page bore a drawing of a dragon crouched on top of a tiny planet, claws grasping the spires of spindly mountains. With a blast of fire, he fended off an in-coming spaceship and its long-nosed cannons.

Noah threw his arms out, grinning idiotically. "Good news!" he said. "I'm here!"

In the silence that followed, the pull cords for the window blinds tapped against the walls. I stopped scrubbing and stared at him, my face blank.

He glanced up and down the boat and dropped his arms. He lowered an eyebrow as if he were half kidding, half trying to sort out if he needed to be serious. "Wow, did somebody die?"

His words jabbed so hard and fast, I almost broke into sobs right there. Instead, I glared at him. "Yeah, actually." I have no idea what made me say it. I guess it felt safer to be angry than to cry.

"Oh." His expression crashed and his shoulders went slack. "Wow, I'm sorry. I had no idea. Who was it?"

Well, gee, that wasn't complicated at all. *I don't know—some dude I'd never met before.* Tears wetting my eyes, I simply bit my lips together and shook my head.

He nodded. "I'm really sorry Bailey." He thumbed his nose and glanced at me from the tops of his eyes. "Hey, if you need anything...?"

Oh, God, drop it already. It was nothing like he thought. I turned and blasted cleaner all over the next window.

He pushed his hands into his back pockets and bounced on his heels. "Well, I guess I'll just..." He nodded his head toward the office barge, tied up at the next pier. "...grab the snacks."

When I didn't reply, he took one sliding step backwards, then slipped out of the boat. He walked down the pier with his head hanging, pausing to kick a loose chip of paint sticking up from the boards.

I sighed and thunked my forehead against the window, cleaning fluid and all. It felt slippery and oozed around my skin. Everything here was wrong. There was no chatter. No joking. No laughing. It was like someone had turned the Mailboat upside down. Like we were all hanging from the floor by the rings in the hatches, and the fish were swimming in through the windows, and we couldn't breathe.

An hour later, I had cleaned every window on the boat before I was finally free to escape to the post office and collect the mail. I shoved the cleaner back into the cupboard and had nearly slipped away when I spied an empty roll of paper towel I'd left on the counter up front. Tommy would flag me if he caught me leaving a mess.

With Tommy fussing over something on the instrument panel, I tried to sneak in quick and grab the offending tube of cardboard before he could notice. I snatched it up, and that's when the stack of newspapers beside it—and the blazing headline—jumped out at me: HOMICIDE VICTIMS IDENTIFIED.

My heart screeched to a stop as all the memories slammed back into my head. I fumbled the paper towel tube and it bounced on the floor.

I glanced at Tommy, but he didn't seem to have noticed. He stood at his helm working a grungy rag around the brass fixtures on the dash, a bottle of brass polish on the counter beside him.

Well, this was peachy. I was going to have to face that headline over and over as I wrapped it around dozens of stacks of mail. Then again, the irony didn't escape me. I was probably *in* that article—*police have questioned an eyewitness*—and here I was delivering it all over the lake.

Wait. Victims identified? I could simply read a newspaper and learn his name. The man with the wavy hair. My heart started beating again, and when it did, it beat hard.

I slid the top newspaper off the stack and began to read.

Police are investigating the deaths of two men who were shot Friday night...

I scanned past the initial summary. I knew that part. Way better than any reporter did. I skipped to the paragraph where they named the two people who had died. One, they said, was Lake Geneva resident Charles Hart, age seventy-three.

I frowned down at the page. Oh my God, I knew who he was. I laid my hand on the stack of newspapers and slid them sideways so I could see the tops. The paper I wanted was towards the very bottom. Tommy had scrawled the names of the recipients in the margins. There it was. *Hart.*

I delivered mail for the guy. Bills and crap. Newspapers—including this one. I hadn't even recognized him the night of the shooting. Then again, you don't expect to be nearly killed by some random guy on your route. I mean, he'd had half his head blown off by the time I got a good look at him. Under the circumstances, why were we even delivering stuff to him anymore? Apparently, stopping your mail wasn't a top priority when you were dead.

I found my place in the article again and looked for the other name. The name of the man I'd wanted so bad to save. I breathed deeply and bit my lips together.

Jason.

Jason Thomlin, age forty-five.

I closed my eyes and pictured him, leaning on his elbows over a cup of coffee and a sandwich. I wrapped the name around him. *Jason.* It felt like the right name for him. Like it couldn't have been any other.

My eyebrows scrunched together. Wait... Thomlin?

I glanced at Tommy out of the corner of my eye. The open jug of polish on the counter filled the air with a smart, tangy scent and the white rag in his hand picked up smears of gray and green as it lifted the patina to reveal bright brass underneath.

Tommy Thomlin.

133

Realization snapped into place. It was like something I could have known all along, if only it hadn't been lost beneath the waves. Like the steam yacht graveyard at Conference Point, the deepest part of the lake, where the millionaires used to sink their most beautiful yachts so no one else would ever own them. Yet we sailed over them every day, oblivious.

I broke my eyes away from Tommy, my heart in my throat. There had to be something more in this article. Something that would explain.

...Jason Thomlin, age forty-five, wanted by the police in connection with a number of bank burglaries that took place in Chicago, Milwaukee, and Madison in the '90s, and the shooting death of Lake Geneva police officer Sid Kruse in 1997...

I stopped and frowned. No. No, this couldn't be right. This was the guy who'd spent his last breath to save a girl who'd served him a sandwich. But there it was in print, a list of sins so wrong, it wouldn't stay buried in the silt anymore. The truth welled to the surface like the wreckage of a sunken yacht rising again, beams half-rotted, lake weed dripping off the roof, water pouring from the deck in a hundred fountains. And there she sat, all shocking and true, and all I could do was stare, mouth gaping.

I glanced again at Tommy. This explained... everything. For the second time that morning, I worked up the nerve to open my mouth. Somehow, it wasn't as hard this time. I had to know.

"Tommy?"

He turned. "Yes, ma'am?" His tone was playful, his smile fake. He probably expected any run-of-the-mill question, like where the canceling stamp had gotten to or what to do if a newspaper was torn.

I held up the paper.

His eyes dropped to the headline, all fat and loud with black ink. He flinched—as if someone had kicked him in the

134

stomach. He jerked his head around to his gauges and polished them hard. His eyes looked stormy with a fifty percent chance of rain.

Oh, God. No wonder. I tried to balance everything I suddenly knew about the man who'd died and my head wanted to explode. He'd been a crook. A killer. A fugitive. He'd tipped me a hundred dollars—probably stolen, now that I thought about it.

And he was related to Tommy.

He was one of the smiling faces I'd imagined for so long, but no longer smiling. The image of the dozen people I'd tied to Tommy's wedding band faltered, like static breaking up a signal. Their grins wavered. Their eyes turned sad. Maybe their lives weren't as idyllic as I liked to imagine.

Okay, now what was I supposed to say? I was never exactly an expert on delicate social situations—and this one was leagues over my head. Not to mention Tommy looked like he was going to cry, which scared the crap out of me. But I couldn't just drop the whole thing and walk away.

"Who was he?" I asked in a whisper.

Tommy crumpled the rag in his hand and leaned on the panel. He tilted his head and opened his mouth, but nothing came out. My question hung abandoned. I couldn't imagine how he felt.

Finally, he answered, in a voice all washed-up and sun-bleached. "He was my son."

My heart cracked. The man with the wavy hair was... Tommy's son.

"Oh. Wow," I said. Okay, *that* was clearly not the socially correct response. I wanted to slap myself.

Tommy bowed his head, but I could still see the corner of his eye, glistening like lake water.

I thumbed the edge of the newspaper. Tommy was standing there trying not to cry, and it was my fault for being nosy. Great. Now what? I could pick up an injured mouse and hold it close and tell it everything was going to be okay. But what the heck was I supposed to say to Tommy? *Gee, that sucks. Hey, point of interest—I was there when it happened.*

Yeah, there was no good way to bring up that conversation. Come to think of it, the mouse had died, anyway.

But the necklace. The necklace belonged with Tommy, not me. Maybe that's why the man with the wavy hair had given it to me. I reached into my pocket.

But Tommy lifted his head. "Bailey... there's something you oughta know..." His voice was low and gravely, as if the words were hard to drum up. As if they'd been sitting on the bottom of the lake with the sunken yachts.

Footsteps echoed down the pier. Voices. Laughter. More of our co-workers were arriving to prep the other boats. Michaela swung through the door into the Mailboat and called up the stairs to Noah on the aft deck. "Noah! I know you guys took the good mop last night! Cough it up."

Tommy glanced over his shoulder at her, then closed his eyes and sighed.

"Um... you gonna be okay?" I whispered.

He lifted half a smile. "I'll be okay." He reached out and chucked me under the chin. His misty eyes met mine and warmed.

I froze.

Was it just me, or was that a hairline crack in the toy shop window?

I suddenly felt the urge to run—which didn't make a lick of sense, and I knew it.

Tommy screwed the lid back on the brass polish and walked away, leaving me standing with the newspaper in my hand, staring after him, my body paralyzed but my mind whirling out of control.

CHAPTER TWENTY-SIX
JIMMY

Jimmy waited on the Riviera pier, checking his atomic watch approximately every fifteen seconds. The Mailboat was due at precisely 12:30 p.m. according to the lady at the ticket booth, and it was already 12:33:45. Jimmy had bypassed the string of people waiting for the next tour and stood beside the gangplank, bouncing on the balls of his feet. Several people gave him dirty looks, no doubt assuming he had cut ahead of the line. He simply scowled back at them. One should never assume. Any scientist knew that.

A horn blast triggered him to jump and turn toward the sound. The Mailboat rounded a larger vessel at the end of the pier and slid in towards its berth.

Near the bow stood exactly the young man Jimmy had hoped to find: Noah Cadigan. Gripping a rail on the side of the boat, Cadigan hung lazily over the lake, a weighty rope slung through his hand. Some might term it a casual pose, considering there was nothing but a catwalk beneath his feet and roughly three meters of water below that. But that was generally Noah Cadigan's way.

He and Jimmy attended a few of the same advanced classes in school. Even more remarkable, Cadigan often caught up with him in the hall to debate things like string theory, manned missions to Mars, and evolutionary development on other planets. At last, someone only a few levels below Jimmy's own intellect. The kid lacked discipline, though. Jimmy frequently caught the young man doodling in class and carrying around works of pure, pseudo-scientific fantasy like *The Martian.* Ninety-nine percent accuracy did not a reliable source make. Jimmy had tired of debating that book with him—and others. What a waste of a sharp mind.

Still, Cadigan might have his strengths. He was what everyone called "a good kid," and the entire school liked him, both students and teachers. Given that, Jimmy could think of no better individual to interview for his current research: How to think with the heart.

Perhaps more to the point, Cadigan was the only person willing to hold a conversation with him. The rest of Jimmy's schoolmates either shunned him or set booby traps in his locker, involving painfully simplistic mechanical devices armed with make-do projectiles such as shaving cream and toilet paper.

The Mailboat pulled up alongside the pier and Cadigan waved with the rope. "Hey, Jimmy."

Jimmy nodded succinctly, hands clasped behind his back, and rocked on his heels some more.

Cadigan jumped off as the boat came within inches of the dock, then bent down to tie his rope to a metal bracket mounted to the wooden boards.

Jimmy stepped up and spoke to the back of his head. "Cadigan, I'm here to have a word with you."

Cadigan rose and brushed his palms on his shorts. He looked at Jimmy with one eyebrow raised. "Is this about wind pressure on the surface of Mars?"

"What? No."

"Inter-galactic travel at the speed of light?"

"I believe I made it clear, I refuse to discuss any form of quote-unquote 'science' proposed by the *Star Wars* franchise."

"The possibility of shape-shifting clowns living in storm drains?"

Jimmy stared. "I beg your pardon?"

"Never mind." Cadigan grinned and shrugged. "What up?"

"I would like to interview you."

"'Interview.'" Cadigan frowned. "Is this going to take a while? 'Cuz I'm working, actually." He gestured toward the boat with an apologetic shrug.

Jimmy flapped his hand. "Minor details. This research can't wait." He extracted a digital recorder from his pocket. "You don't mind if I record our conversation, do you?" He flicked the switch and positioned it a few degrees below Cadigan's nose.

Cadigan flinched backwards. "Oh. Um..." He shrugged. "I... guess that's okay. Can we talk while I work?"

"Certainly," Jimmy agreed with a nod. It was less than ideal; he would have preferred his subject's undivided attention. But a true scientist adapted to the circumstances. As Cadigan bent down to tighten the rope, Jimmy followed his movement to reposition the recorder beneath his nose. "So, first question: How does one think with the heart?"

Cadigan looked up, brows arching, eyes unnaturally wide. "Huh?"

Jimmy drew impatient little circles with the recorder. "How does one think with the heart?"

Mouth slack, Cadigan offered a blank stare. "Remind me why you won't discuss *Star Wars?*"

Jimmy huffed and dropped the device to his side. "I'm endeavoring to conduct a serious conversation here."

"Okay, sorry." Cadigan smothered a grin. "One second," he said, lifting a finger. "I gotta help with the gangway. And then we'll return to this... serious conversation."

Jimmy was sure he caught laughter as Cadigan turned away.

After assisting with the gangway, Cadigan took up a post at the end. A stream of tourists flowed out of the boat and he thanked each of them for coming and offered one and all a broad smile.

Jimmy stepped aside to avoid the stream of traffic and lifted his recorder to his mouth. "Wednesday, June twenty-fifth," he said, "twelve thirty-seven p.m. The subject, Noah Cadigan, male, sixteen, bares his teeth, and this is somehow interpreted by the populace as a friendly gesture."

Some eleven and a half minutes later, the final tourist was gone. Cadigan beckoned for Jimmy, who stepped across the gangway and followed Cadigan to the front of the boat. Cadigan began to sort bags and boxes full of mail.

"Want to come with me to the post office?" Cadigan asked. "I've got to drop off the mail and be back in time for the next tour."

"Ah... very well." In hindsight, catching Cadigan at work had been a bad idea.

Jimmy's interviewee deftly canceled stamps on a stack of envelopes. "So, where were we?"

Jimmy leaned in closer, lifted the recorder, and repeated his question softly, hopeful no one else would hear. Based on Cadigan's humored reaction, he wasn't quite as certain about the direction of this interview. "Um... I just wanted to know how one thinks with the heart."

Cadigan twirled the canceling stamp in the air and squinted with one eye. "Is this a trick question?"

"No, it's—" Jimmy choked. What was he trying to say? He wasn't sure. Perhaps he was misusing his terminology—such a beginner mistake in any field, he had never before made it. His pulse accelerated so violently, he could feel the contractions of his heart through his rib cage.

Cadigan beheld him with a studied expression, then smiled subtly and stamped his last envelope. "Oh," he said. "I think I know what you're trying to get at." He closed the cover on the ink pad.

"You do?" Jimmy felt relief wash over him.

Cadigan nodded and tossed his remaining envelopes into a white cardboard box bearing the emblem of the US Postal Service. "In answer to your question: the way to 'think' with your heart, as you put it..." He looked Jimmy in the eye. His own shined like an incandescent bulb. "...is to open your heart up." He cupped his hands together and made an opening gesture, like a book.

Jimmy's jaw dropped. "Open-heart surgery? Granted, I haven't read many studies, but—"

Cadigan sighed and rolled his eyes. "I don't mean *literally.* Look, when talking about stuff like this, you can't be literal."

"Then I see no point in carrying on this conversation."

"Not everything can be measured with a beaker, Jimmy."

"Of course not. That's why we have digital scales and graduated cylinders and stage micrometers, to say nothing of mass spectrometers and—"

Cadigan sighed and elevated his brows. "Oh, boy." He hauled a box of mail off the counter top, balanced it on his hip, and made for the open window facing the pier.

Jimmy frowned at the canceling stamp and a small plastic bag full of rubber bands. There must be some way to salvage this interview. Screwing up his face, he gamely followed his subject, who was now tossing the mail through the window onto the pier. To Jimmy's surprise, Cadigan went through the window after it. Hence, so did Jimmy. On the pier, Cadigan transferred his bags and boxes to a large blue handcart.

Jimmy stuck the recorder in Cadigan's face again. "Let me propose a hypothetical situation."

"Hypothesize away," Cadigan said.

"Say a young male entering reproductive maturity is attracted to a young female who is also entering reproductive maturity."

"'Reproductive maturity?'" Cadigan repeated. "Wait." He narrowed an eye and grinned. "Are you wondering how babies are made?"

Jimmy flushed. "No! I only use the term as an indicator of the approximate age of the subjects under study."

Cadigan puffed his cheeks, shaking his head. "Wow. Okay."

"I understand the various courtship rituals: Flowers, candy, movies, dinner, or possibly coffee for a more casual, not to mention mature, approach. But what exactly dictates the female's response? Why will she reject one potential mate in preference for the other?"

Cadigan laughed. "If I knew that, I'd never again be crashed in a beanbag with my kid brother, watching the entire *Cars* series on repeat."

Jimmy frowned. "I'm sorry. I don't understand your answer."

Cadigan folded his arms over the edge of the blue cart. "Look, it has nothing to do with formulas. Sometimes people click, sometimes they don't. That's all there is to it. You just gotta try. You know, screw up your courage and ask the girl."

"I have."

Cadigan jerked his head back. "You *have?* Wow. How'd it go?"

Jimmy stared at him blankly. "Had the desired outcome been achieved, the present interview would be rendered extraneous."

Cadigan thumped the cart with his thumbs and nodded. "Noted." He began to wheel his cart up the pier.

Jimmy scrambled to keep up with him, recorder extended. "Surely there's a way to increase the odds of success? For instance, does evidence exist suggesting that one variety of flower is more successful than another? Roses as opposed to carnations, as an example?"

Cadigan shrugged as he navigated the crowded pier. "Depends what the girl likes. But honestly, if she turned me down because I brought the wrong flower, I'd say she's the wrong girl."

"But what if one doesn't know the female's preference?"

"Then ask her."

Jimmy stopped dead, a sensation as cold as absolute zero creeping through his circulatory system. *"Ask her?"*

Cadigan pulled up and glanced back. "Sure, why not?"

Because it sounded like yet another phenomenal way to to embarrass himself, that was why not. Jimmy scrunched his face in thought. "No, I have a better plan. The scientific method. I shall run a new series of experiments: Offer a rose, and observe the reaction. If the rose theorem is proved false, try the carnation. And so forth."

Cadigan lifted a brow as his jaw went slack. "Umm..."

"Of course! How simple!" Jimmy paced as the design for the experiment came clear. "I wonder, will one of each varietal suffice? No, hardly. I would also need to test the effects of one flower versus multiples—say up to a dozen. I suppose I should also stock one of each color..."

Cadigan ground his face into his palm.

Jimmy ceased pacing. "You appear distressed."

"Look." He bounced his upturned palms, as if seeking the comparative weights of two items that did not exist. "I don't think you should go through with that experiment."

"Why not?"

"Just—trust me on this one. *Please.*"

"What do you propose instead?"

Cadigan spread his hands. "Tell her how you feel. Why you want to go out with her."

"Well, that's simple. I've run the probabilities on the success of our relationship, and statistically speaking—"

"No."

Cadigan placed a hand on Jimmy's shoulder. The gesture was so unexpected and performed with such intensity that Jimmy found himself wordlessly glancing down at the intruding limb. Its presence was unnerving, but surprisingly not unwelcome. When he re-established eye contact, Cadigan was staring at him firmly.

"How do you feel when she walks into a room?" Cadigan asked. "How do you feel *inside?*"

Jimmy stared into the intense blue eyes—intense not in terms of color saturation or the visible light spectrum. In fact, the hue was relatively washed-out, like a faded photograph of a once-blue ocean. Rather, the severity of Cadigan's expression appeared to come from something that arose from inside the human being that was Noah Cadigan and expressed itself through the eyes. For the first time in his life, Jimmy thought he understood the poetic expression, *windows to the soul.*

Jimmy considered Cadigan's question. He pictured Bailey bustling around the restaurant, arms laden with steaming dishes. Or Bailey curled up in a chair at the school library, her nose buried in the pages of a book.

"I feel..." he stuttered, "like all the darkness has been sucked away, and there's nothing left but sunlight and flowers and singing birds."

His own words startled him. They sounded as unscientific as words possibly could. But there was no other way to describe how he felt around Bailey. He felt the way he had long ago, before the darkness had come. Back when life was full of cartwheels and Queen Anne's lace and angel-winged butterflies, bursting with color, fanning themselves on his sister's palm as she giggled.

"I feel happy," Jimmy finished.

Cadigan's eyes softened. His lips spread into a smile—full of warmth, as if the two of them were connected by more than just the hand on Jimmy's shoulder. "*That* is what you should tell her."

A tremor raced through Jimmy's entire body, from his feet to the nape of his neck and back down again. "She won't laugh at me?"

"Hey, that's every guy's fear." He shrugged. "If she does, laugh back and walk away. There's some other girl out there for you." He shrugged. "Anyway, that's what my old man tells me."

Jimmy nodded and stared at his shoes. This was the same way he had felt speaking with Roland Markham—a quietude mixed with massive shots of terror. And suddenly, he understood what the old man meant by *thinking with your heart.* He hadn't expected it to be so intense. So beautiful. So painful.

He swallowed back the lump in his throat. "Thank you."

Cadigan grinned and nodded. "Hey, any time."

Jimmy cleared his throat and squared his shoulders, grasping for his usual poise. He tugged on the tails of his tee shirt, as if to straighten the wrinkles he'd already ironed that morning. "Your name will, of course, appear in the study upon its publication."

Cadigan screwed up his face. "Wait, you're publishing all this?"

"All studies must face peer review in a respected scientific journal."

Cadigan shifted his weight and tapped a foot. "So, next question: Have you ever been published in a scientific journal?"

"As of yet, no."

He grinned. "Okay, then I'm not worried." He swatted Jimmy on the shoulder. "Good luck. Let me know how it goes, all right?"

"Certainly."

Cadigan removed his mobile device from his pocket and checked the screen. "Hey, I gotta run. Take it easy, man. We'll catch up later." With a wave of his hand, he threw his weight against the pushcart and jogged down the quay.

Jimmy watched him go. The interview had left him feeling like an empty beaker, the contents spilled across the lab floor. He had a lot of thinking to do. About Bailey. About *The Master Plan.* About the Backfire Model. Maybe even about his sister.

He cleared his throat and bounced on his heels. One arm folded behind his back, he smartly clicked the button on his recorder, only to see a light blink on, not off.

Crap. He hadn't recorded a thing.

CHAPTER TWENTY-SEVEN
TOMMY

There was no need to don suit or tie for this occasion. I showed up at the cemetery in my captain's uniform after my last tour. No one was here except me, the grounds keeper, and of course Jason.

I hadn't told Bailey I was burying her father today. Maybe I should have. I almost had this morning. I almost told her she'd *had* a father. At the last minute, I'd bailed on her.

I'd done that twice now.

It was selfish of me.

I just wanted to be alone.

The grounds keeper finished adjusting the straps around the casket and laid his hand on the winch. He paused and tugged on the brim of his dusty cap. "Uh... If you'd like a last—"

"No," I said.

He stared at me and blinked, his brow and his mouth two hard lines. This cemetery dated to the Civil War, and I often wondered if he did, too. We'd crossed paths often enough, when I came to decorate my wife's grave. He would lean on his trimmer and talk as if he'd known her—or rather, as if he still knew her. *What've you there? Lilies? Oh, those are her favorite, for sure.* In fairness, he talked that way about all the tenants of the graveyard. *Me an' Abe over there was just talkin' about our favorite spots to go fishin'.* Abe had been dead a hundred years.

Funerals made the old grounds keeper happy—another resident to keep him company. Jason's lack of ceremony clearly wasn't sitting well.

He coughed into his fist and rolled his shoulders, as if adjusting a suit rather than suspenders. He followed that gesture up with a clasping of his hands, a brief bow of his head, and a solemn stare into the hole, as if someone here present ought to observe something resembling the rites of burial. Finally, he turned on the winch. The casket lowered into the ground.

Another car crunched on the gravel road several yards away. I ignored it, anticipating other mourners paying respects to other deceased. Instead, the doors popped open and the two occupants strolled between the headstones, wending their way toward me hand-in-arm.

"Tommy," Wade said with a nod.

He was in uniform. Just dropping by after work. Same as me. His wife Nancy was the only one who had apparently gone out of her way for the occasion. The white pencil skirt, floral blouse, and heels were more than she typically wore to her job as a museum docent. She was even carrying a rose. She flashed me a smile, which I didn't return.

We all faced the grave and didn't speak. There was nothing to be said. The winch whirred and groaned slowly, like something dying, until the casket touched bottom. The grounds keeper removed the straps, followed by the scaffold, all of which he threw into the back of a waiting pickup.

He glanced at us uncertainly. "Uh… If you'd like a few minutes…"

I shook my head no.

He rubbed behind his ear. "I, uh… I gotta bring in the Bobcat," he said.

I raised my eyebrows and swept a hand in invitation. "Go ahead."

He yanked off his Packers cap and scratched his head, muttering as he walked away. "No self-respecting mourners that I have ever…" He tromped across the cemetery to the flatbed trailer waiting on the road.

"You're welcome to come to our place tonight," Wade said. He stared at the hole, not me, as if eye contact might be unwelcome.

"Thanks," I said.

Nancy touched my arm and smiled. "You'll come?"

I didn't cushion it. "No."

Her face fell, but she let her hand slide away. "Our door is always open, Tommy," she said with a last squeeze of my hand.

I nodded.

The Bobcat rumbled into action, crawled down the ramp from the flatbed, and picked its way through the tombstones. Odd to think that the miracle of life ends with the wonder of a skid steer loader. No mystery why most people leave before this part. We'd prefer to die with dignity—even if we failed to live with it.

The machine drowned out further conversation—thankfully. We watched as the grounds keeper poured crushing piles of earth over my son and tamped it down with the bucket, as if to lock him in place. When the job was done, a compact mound of dirt rose out of a bed of matted grass. The skid steer rumbled back to its trailer.

This was not how my son ought to have been buried, and I knew it. Even with all the bad blood between us, this should not have been how we said good-bye.

But neither should he have died in the first place.

With the Bobcat gone, the sound of birds and grasshoppers returned. It was about the right time for someone to offer stirring words. Instead, I stared at the mound, wishing Wade and his wife would say whatever platitudes they'd come to offer and leave. This burial was not about mourning the premature loss of a son. It was not a heart-broken good-bye. It was not a tearful sending off into the next life. It was a hiding away of something that had gone embarrassingly wrong. A sweeping under the rug. A chance to say, "Well, that didn't turn out as planned."

Nancy bobbed her head briefly, her blond hair, pinned up in a messy twist, catching a ray of sunlight. She stepped forward, got down on her knees in the dirt-strewn grass, and laid the rose on top of the mound. Then she transferred a kiss from her fingertips to the pile of earth. Her hand splayed gently, as if touching Jason himself, and she muttered, "Be at peace, Jason. You're home now."

A hitch caught at my throat, but I said nothing.

While she was there, she took a moment to greet Laina, my wife, by laying a hand on her headstone. "You're still missed, Elaina," she said. "Look out for Jason." After a moment of silence, the breeze playing with the sheer ruffles on her sleeves, she rose and threaded her arm through Wade's again.

I supposed I ought to say something. "Thank you," I scratched out.

A smile creased her lips. "Of course."

The grounds keeper came back for his pickup. He paused and motioned uncertainly towards the grave. "If there's anything special you'd like done..."

I sighed. He had to have known by now that it was a pointless suggestion. "No," I said patiently. "The temporary marker, as we discussed."

He nodded and shuffled towards his truck. "Well... have a nice day."

It was honestly the most appropriate thing he'd said this whole time. The door creaked and banged, the truck lurched into gear, and he drove off to hitch the flatbed.

Wade gripped my shoulder. "I'll stop by later this week. See how you're getting along."

I nodded resignedly. There was no convincing him to let it lie. That all I wanted was to move on.

"Call us if you need anything."

"Sure."

Wade gave my shoulder a parting squeeze. Nancy hugged me lightly. And they finally left, arm-in-arm, through the tombstones. I waited until their car was out of sight. Until no one was left but me and the dead. The entire Thomlin family was present and accounted for. Together again at last.

I shoved my hands into my pockets and tilted my head at my son, a thousand unanswered questions crowding their way into my mouth. "Why did you...?" I stopped myself. I shouldn't open with an accusation. I licked my lips and tried again. "Where did I go wrong?"

The mound of earth didn't reply.

I shook the endless questions out of my head. No sense even thinking about it anymore. It was over. Past.

As if Jason had never happened.

I stepped towards Laina's tombstone and lowered creakily to my knee. The grass was a bit ragged around our headstone—hers and mine. I pulled away the bits that should have been caught by the trimmer. It would be her birthday soon. I would bring a wreath of lilies, as I did every year.

"Well," I said to her, still plucking grass. "He came home."

If a grave could smile, I thought perhaps it did. Maybe they were together now, Laina and Jason. I knew she would welcome him with arms wide. She'd never been able to stay mad at anyone more than an hour or two. Especially our son.

"Did he give you the helm?" I asked her. "He was supposed to bring it back."

The tombs were silent.

Wade had already given me a cardboard box containing the personal affects not considered relevant to the investigation. The silver helm was not among them. It was as I thought. Jason had lost it years ago. Or thrown it away. It hadn't meant enough to him to keep it safe. But it didn't matter anymore. The silver helm had always existed to bring us home to each other. Now, there was no one else to bring home.

That wasn't true.

I sighed shakily. Looking at Laina, I cocked my head toward Jason. "He has something to tell you. Make sure he does. All those beautiful grandchildren you hoped for..."

I bowed my head, unable to finish the thought. A vise latched onto my soul and squeezed. The dreams Laina and I had had for our family had gone off in every which-way. Yes, Jason had come home. Yes, we had a grandchild. But it was all wrong. It was all wrong...

I covered my eyes and wept.

THURSDAY
JUNE 26, 2014

CHAPTER TWENTY-EIGHT
BUD

It was a cold, damp morning, like a two-day-old sandwich forgotten in the cooler. Hunkered behind a wooden locker on the Mailboat pier, Bud tried to shuffle his feet without either blowing his cover or tripping backwards into the lake. It had seemed like a good hiding place ten minutes ago. He was within spitting distance of the boat. But now, as he tried to get circulation down past his knees and through his burning calves, he cussed himself out for not choosing a more comfortable hiding spot. The damned pier offered precious few opportunities for a six-foot-two, couple-a-hundred-and-eighty-pound dude.

Still, Bud felt a weighty sense of solemnity in his bones. Or maybe that was just the effects of gravity on his beer gut after an eternity in a cramped position. Damn it, he wished the old man would hurry up and make a showing. He checked his watch again. Should be any minute.

After hanging around the Riviera and the docks for so many days, he'd decided that somewhere on the pier was the best angle from which to make his entrance. He was closer to the boat here on the dock than he would have been on the street, but he could still observe his target from a safe distance. He could see through the windows on the lower deck, too. He'd be able to track his subject's movements and close in at the perfect moment.

He'd gotten everything ready the night before. The Riv was bristling with security cameras. Those were disabled now. A BB gun had done the trick. To prevent the cameras from capturing his image in the last moments of their life, he had worn his good ol' baseball cap rigged with LED lights. The only image on those cameras would be a blob of white, then blackness as he shot out their electronic eyes.

He'd taken his time about the whole thing, Sunday driver style. The BB gun was back at home now, along with the LED cap. He'd even grabbed a couple hours of shut-eye. Then, as the sun started to bleed all over the eastern sky, he'd pulled on his favorite black leather vest and driven to within a few blocks of ground zero, parked in a security camera blind zone, and strolled down the street as if he had nothing to do but kill time.

He shuffled his feet again and reached inside his vest to finger the smooth, polymer grip of the .22 rimfire. He'd chosen the Little Babe for this job. A gig like this didn't call for a high level of stopping power. Not for what he had in mind. Concealment was bigger on his list of priorities. The Babe fit inside his waistband and under his vest as if it wasn't even there. Quiet little thing, too. It was the same piece he'd used to finish off Jason Thomlin. How did the saying go? Like father, like son.

Footsteps echoed on the wooden boards. The rift in the silence electrified Bud like gunfire. He peered around his locker to see the old man walking down the pier, canvas rucksack and all. He was a full twenty minutes before the hour and the only other living thing in sight.

Bud grinned.

CHAPTER TWENTY-NINE
TOMMY

You can only lie in bed staring at the ceiling for so long. Eventually you just need to get up and do something so you can quit thinking. I'd been coming to the Mailboat earlier every day. But it's hard to run away from yourself. My thoughts never failed to follow me.

I unlocked the doors, set my rucksack on a chair, and took the glass insert out of the mail jumper's window to let in the fresh air. I'd started every summer morning this way for nearly half a century. There was solace in the routine. Come what may, I would unlock the doors, set down my rucksack, and open the window. I leaned the glass insert in its usual place on the opposite side of the boat, then pulled off my jacket and folded it across the back of the pilot's chair. Its armrests were well-smoothed, its vinyl seat softened and cracked.

Slowly, I stepped up to the helm and gripped the cool wood. Felt it warm under my hands. Listened to the waves lapping the hull. Forty-five years ago, a much younger me had stood behind this same wheel, beaming with pride, wanting to boast to the world that I'd just become a father. I never dreamed I'd see the day my son died.

The Mailboat had seen me through everything before, good and bad. I ran my fingers over the wheel. It bore a patina from fifty years of my own sweat and skin oil. She was in my soul, and I was in hers. She was an extension of my hands and feet. I could feel a ripple through her hull and the effects of a breeze through her floorboards. She was more than a seventy-five-foot tour boat. She was my lifeblood. I tightened my hands around the spokes, closed my eyes, and asked my old friend to leech the pain away. But she felt silent to me. Detached. Perhaps it was too great a burden to ask of her. She wouldn't become a party to my sins.

"Come back, Jason," I whispered, the pain wrenching inside my chest. "Come back. I'm sorry." I covered my eyes and let the tears flow.

Footsteps beat hollowly on the wooden pier. I turned my face away. *What are you doing here, Bailey? Don't see me like this.*

It was early. Very early. We had the boat and the piers to ourselves for a long while yet. A small but firm voice told me I had every opportunity right now to tell her. To tell her about her father. To tell her everything. She was far ahead of her usual time.

Which did beg the question... What was she doing here?

The boat rocked, yawing deeply to starboard, as someone stepped through the door.

I lowered my hand and opened my eyes. It wasn't Bailey. She was too small to rock the boat.

A heavy footstep halted midship. "You Tommy?"

I didn't know that voice. I didn't like it, either. He dished out my name like a four-letter word. Slowly, I turned.

The sunrise glowed around the blurred edges of a bulky silhouette. I lifted a hand to shade my eyes, but to no avail. The sunbeams shot around his form like the glory of an angel and and glinted strangely with silver points of light.

"Are you Tommy?" he asked again, laying emphasis on every word. The messengers of God were not to be toyed with.

I dropped my hand to my side and let the light blind me. "Yes," I replied.

The head nodded in satisfaction. "I have something for you."

My heart beat harder. With barely half a dozen words passed between us, I understood. I knew what it was he'd come to give me. I didn't bother to ask why. Knowing was enough.

I straightened my shoulders and let the thought sink in. I hadn't started my day expecting to die. But in hindsight, I simply hadn't known that I'd known. This, then, was how it had always been meant to end. There was no fear. Instead, this new and final turn in my life brought a sense of peace, like thunder over fields desperate for rain. I was ready for this. I wanted this. I'd been wanting it for a long time now.

"You... killed my son." It wasn't a question.

The head bobbed. "Tough nut to crack, that kid. He went down blazin'. You should be proud of him."

Proud of him. A corner of my mouth flinched. The jab dug deep.

I squinted into the light. "Who are you?" If he was going to kill me, it would be nice to know his name.

He shook his head dismissively, like a dog shaking an unpleasant morsel out of its mouth. "It's like I said." He shuffled a step forward. "I got somethin' for you." As his body briefly eclipsed the sun, I glimpsed an unshaved face. An arm scarred with tattoos. A black leather vest. A grim apparition—but not as black as my own soul. He planted his feet again and blended into the light.

I licked my lips slowly. Nodded. There was no reason to drag this out; no sense clinging to explanations.

In my pride, I may have anticipated being escorted through the waters by no less than an archangel. I knew now I deserved no such honors. This fallen specimen was the best God could spare me. But now was not the time or place to register complaints. Here was my angel of vengeance, and I accepted that he had been sent to repay my sins.

"Okay," I said in a low voice. "Then I guess you'd better give it to me."

I felt his eyes on me. Weighing me. Measuring me in the balance. Finding me wanting.

"You aren't scared," he observed.

Cold sweat poured down my back, but I didn't baulk. "No."

He nodded. His voice dripped from his lips in a pure, distilled hate. "Then Mary, Joe, and Jesus, I'll *make* you scared."

He slid into a ready stance, feet spread. He reached into his vest. Both hands came together in a two-handed grip, grasping a pistol between them. I breathed deeply and closed my eyes just as his finger tightened down on the trigger and the first flash seared from the muzzle. By a change in air pressure, a puff of wind, I sensed a hard, hot ball pass within inches of my face. Glass cracked. Infinitesimal shards, like needles, like ice, rained down on the back of my neck. The gun spit again. Lead hit wood with a *thluck*, as if a wounded slab of pine had pulled in a sharp gasp. Chips and splinters pelted my hands and the backs of my legs. The boat took a third round with a brittle crack of plastic, the snap of tiny electric arcs.

Auditory exclusion. According to Wade, you weren't supposed to hear a thing during an exchange of gunfire. The effects of adrenaline. Of fight-or-flight. Your body shuts down anything it doesn't absolutely need to survive.

I didn't need to survive. I heard every bullet.

MAILBOAT II

"You scared yet, old man? You scared yet? You scared yet?"

I opened my eyes. The black mouth of the barrel stared at me hollowly. Hungrily. I waited, ready to greet what it had to give me.

The man dropped his arms and straightened to his full height. "Damn you. What's it take, anyway?" With a careless flip of his wrist, he pointed the gun and yanked the trigger.

The slug hammered me below the rib.

I dropped.

The smell of lemon floor cleaner filled my nostrils. The pain was hot. White hot. As if I'd been stabbed in the gut with a burning brand. The boat was suddenly silent except for the sound of my own breathing. Ragged. Agonized. Face-down, I writhed.

The floorboards heaved under the weight of his footsteps as he closed in. A shadow leaned over me. His breath smelled like liquor. He touched the hot barrel of the gun to my jaw and drew it up across my cheek, searing.

"Want any more, Tommy?" he crooned.

With a single word of assent, I could swiftly draw the curtains together on a life that had gone badly. I could take my final bow, without having pulled the trigger myself. I could leave my life where I had spent so much of it, on the Mailboat. Yes. I wanted more. I wanted everything left in the magazine. I grit my teeth against the pain. "Please..."

He laughed, perhaps mistaking my murmurings as a plea for mercy. "You'll bleed out before she gets here," he whispered.

My heart slammed into my ribs. God, no. He knew Bailey was coming. What had I done? "Don't hurt her," I gasped.

He chuckled again. "Don't worry, Tommy. I won't."

The man reached down. Grabbed my shoulder. Rolled me onto my side. I groaned. He tilted his meaty head and regarded me studiously, as if admiring his handiwork.

"You sure you don't want another one?" he asked. "Gut wounds are hell. I could put you out of your misery." He brushed the barrel of the gun over the wound. "Or I could let you suffer." He jabbed hard.

I cried out.

"Go ahead and scream, Tommy," he whispered in my ear. "There's nobody else here. Just you and me."

Had Jason suffered like this, too? Had he been tortured and played with before he died? "Why did you kill my son?"

The man shrugged. "Money."

Money? Blind rage nearly obscured the pain. "Is that why you came for me, too? For money?"

"Nah," he said. "This one's personal." He leaned closer, until his cheek brushed mine, and gave me another poke in the side. "That's for interfering with Bailey," he breathed into my ear.

His neck was dotted with sweat. His body heat enveloped me in a stifling cloud. His vest smelled like old leather, old frying oil, and old vomit. Heart racing, I squeezed my eyes shut, trying to block him out.

Warm metal pressed against my forehead.

I gasped and a shudder ran through my entire body. Soon, now. It was almost over. Thank God, it would all be over.

Instead, the gun snapped away.

"You're scared," he said. "Took you frickin' long enough." He sniffed and swiped his arm across his nose. Straightened. Smiled at me. "You know, I like it like this. There's no fun in killin', did'ya know that? I kill you, it's over. But this way?" He smirked and tapped the gun barrel against the wound. I flinched. "You'll never be the same man again, Tommy. I promise you that. Consider this a memento. A reminder. You'll never forget me for as long as you live." He stood and stuffed the gun into his belt. "Which might not be long anyhow."

His footsteps moved toward the door.

I breathed again, a cataclysm of conflicted desires crashing down on me. I wanted him to come back and finish the job. I wanted him to go away before Bailey got here.

He lingered in the doorway, staring back at me. "*If* you live, I'll see ya later," he said. "I promise ya that, Tommy. But I promise you this, too: *You* won't see *me*." He chuckled and made his exit. His footsteps groaned down the pier. Faded away.

He was gone.

Waves of agony rolled over me. I squeezed my eyes shut and dug my fingernails into the floorboards. The man was right. I was gonna bleed out before Bailey got here.

A tear rolled down my cheek. I should have told her. My Bailey-girl. I should have told her...

Bailey-girl. Hurry.

CHAPTER THIRTY
BAILEY

I hiked the strap of my backpack higher up my shoulder and trudged under the archways of the Riviera. I had a funny feeling today was going to be a bad day and I wasn't sure why. Maybe because every day of my life was a bad day. Few exceptions.

Maybe because I'd already taken a huge risk and it was bound to backfire on me.

I was wearing the silver ship's wheel. Like, around my neck.

It made no sense to wear a gift from a man who had broken into banks, stolen millions, and taken someone's life. But maybe it made sense to wear a gift from Tommy's son. In a convoluted way, it was kind of like having Tommy himself right next to my heart.

It felt like one of the most daring things I'd ever done.

Well, not that daring. I was wearing it under my shirt, where no one would know it was there but me.

I sighed and looked where I was going so I wouldn't run into a pier post or something. Or walk off the edge of the dock into the lake. I was prone to dumb stuff like that. No idea how I qualified for a mail jumper.

My eyes landed on the windshield of the Mailboat. That was funny. It looked like it was cracked or something. As I came closer, the sun sparkled off radiating fractures spinning out from the glittering center of a little round hole. Like someone had thrown a rock through the windshield.

Wait. I'd seen those kinds of holes before. In the windshield of Bud's car.

Bullet holes.

No, no, no... what's happening?

I stopped and listened. I didn't hear anything except the lake water lapping the quay.

"Tommy...?" My voice squeaked. The Mailboat door was open. So was the mail jumper's window.

I stepped toward the boat. It was way too quiet around here, except for my pulse pounding in my own ears. The smart shoulder angel told me to run to a safe distance and call the police. My dumb shoulder angel, the one I spent more time with, reminded me that I'd literally rather be shot than have to deal with cops again. Especially Ryan.

I tiptoed forward and peered through the open window. My life ended.

"Tommy!"

I dropped my backpack, swung my legs through the opening, and skidded to my knees beside him. They slipped in something wet. Blood.

He lay sprawled on his side on the floor. His eyes were closed. I shook him by the shoulder. He was limp.

Tears welled in my eyes. This wasn't happening. *No, no, no. Not Tommy. Not Tommy. Take anyone from me but Tommy.*

CHAPTER THIRTY-ONE
TOMMY

I blinked. A forest of white plastic chair legs blurred across my vision. The floor rolled to sickening pitches in fast and slow motion, both at the same time, as if the Mailboat were caught in choppy waters on some psychedelic lake. I needed to get to the helm. But I couldn't clear the fog from my eyes. I couldn't move. It hurt to breathe.

I wasn't alone. I squeezed my eyes shut and opened them again. Tried to focus. A pair of knees. Smeared with blood.

"Tommy? Please, please answer me." Her voice trembled.

I turned toward the sound. A face ringed in wispy brown curls. A wavy ponytail draped over her shoulder.

"Bailey?"

I was answered by a flood of sobs.

I smiled and closed my eyes again. *Bailey-girl.*

My head swam. I'd been shot. I must've passed out. How much blood had I lost?

"Bailey. Listen to me." My words were mumbled and slurred. I forced them through my uncooperative mouth.

"I've been shot. It's… it's bad." My voice snagged on the pain.

She stared at me, unmoving. As if she had turned to stone.

"Bailey?"

She nodded, but that was all.

I closed my eyes against a new wave of agony. Black ice crept in behind it, settling into every bone, every nerve end, every cell of my body. Panic rose in my throat.

I never should have kept the truth from her. I should have told her. I should tell her now. Before I died. I forced my eyes open. Looked up into Bailey's tear-stained face. Fought for the right words.

My eye fell on a tarnished ball chain hanging around her neck, like the one that had held my dog tags a lifetime ago. She'd never worn a chain like that before. Not that I could think of. I followed it down to where it disappeared inside her collar. Whatever was on the end of the chain was on the verge of spilling out as she leaned over me. Gravity teased away at it and finally won. The chain slithered to its full length.

A silver ship's helm dangled and swayed, catching points of light, like a tiny star that shone its brightest in daylight.

I stared, dumbstruck. How had Bailey gotten it? This wasn't possible.

It was.

Jason hadn't lost it after all. No, he'd left it where I was sure to find it. Where I was sure to hear his last request of me. Not my forgiveness. Not my love. Something more. With his death, there was only one Thomlin left adrift at sea.

He was asking me to bring her home.

I fought back tears, the full brunt of my self-centeredness finally hitting home. Keeping the truth from her had been bad enough; merely telling her the truth would never be good enough. I was no help to her dead, any more than her dad was. She needed someone to be there for her. I had no excuse shoving that responsibility off on strangers, on welfare.

I'd left her abandoned too long already.

I breathed. Rallied. Beat back the closing darkness and grabbed hold of the daylight, the star that embraced the sun. Reaching my hand to the raw wound in my side, I touched it gingerly and glanced at my fingers. Not as much blood as I had feared. But the way my head was swimming... the blood loss had to be internal.

"Bailey," I said. "You need to help me. I need you to slow down this bleeding and call for help."

She still didn't move. Her eyes were like a terrified animal.

I tried again. "Do you know how to apply pressure? Didn't they ever show you that in school?"

She glanced at my bloody fingers and her face contorted with fresh tears.

Time was slipping away. Time we didn't have. "Please," I said, the fear creeping into my voice. Fear as much for her as for me. "Bailey-girl. I need you to be brave."

Her eyes shifted and met mine. They finally held the faintest glimmer of clarity. She was here with me now, in this moment, if only barely. Her hand reached to my side. She bit her lips together and slowly pressed into the wound. I tried to breathe slowly and brace myself—

Crucifying pain jolted through my body. I cried out.

Bailey jerked her hand away. She shook her head, six or seven watery trails tracing each cheek. "Tommy—"

I couldn't let the ice creep back in...

"Bailey," I said. "Please." I opened my palm and tried to catch her eye again. "Give me your hand."

She sat staring at me, her mouth gaping. She didn't move.

CHAPTER THIRTY-TWO
BAILEY

I couldn't move. Why couldn't I move? My body was frozen, but my mind was racing.

Wake up, Bailey, wake up. It's a nightmare. This isn't actually happening.

I wanted to slap myself—like, crazy-bitch-slap myself until I snapped out of it. But then if it wasn't a dream, Tommy would think I'd lost it.

I *was* losing it, though. I blinked and my world was dark for a nanosecond—a nanosecond in which I saw a good-looking man with money to fling at waitresses bleeding to death in the street. Tommy's son. A mere hour before he'd been gunned down, I'd daydreamed that whoever this guy was, he had come to finally rescue me. To adopt me. And boom—he was dead.

I'd daydreamed about Tommy, too, and for way longer. Like, ever since I'd first laid eyes on him. My soul had recognized the penultimate father immediately. This was the one. The perfect candidate. Something about him had shattered all the armor-plated walls around my heart, and all my fears that men as a species were cruel brutes who beat you and screwed you and threw you back into your cage when they were done. He was everything I'd ever dreamed of in a dad—or a grandfather—and I had let him inside my heart. I had secretly adopted him. He had no idea, or I hoped to God he didn't. I worshiped the ground he walked on.

I'd let him become my whole world—the reason I went on existing when the other kids were cruel or when Bud was beating the crap out of me. All I had to do was wrap myself in my own arms and pretend they were Tommy's, and I found I could scrape my carcass off the floor and keep trucking, just dreaming of the day Tommy would notice me for real and fold me under his wing and make all the evil go away.

I should have known. I should have known my life was hard-wired for punishment. If I so much as dreamed about a dad, a grandpa, whatever—the guy was toast. Shot. Literally.

Tommy was dying, and it was my fault. It was all my fault.

I sat there frozen, tears streaming down my cheeks. *I'm sorry, Tommy. I won't love you anymore. I'll try so hard. Just please, don't die.*

CHAPTER THIRTY-THREE
TOMMY

Eternal seconds—vital seconds—dragged by, and she didn't move. Just stared at me with the tears streaming down her cheeks. It was too much for her. She was only a child. A child who had already known too much violence, much of it directed at her. She was still wearing long sleeves to cover her latest bruises. She was scared. Of course she was scared.

The boat pitched sickeningly and I closed my eyes, knowing the sensation was only in my head. I felt a buzz in my brain and heard it in my ears, as if everything were short circuiting. I was going to black out again. I knew if I fell asleep, I'd never wake.

"Bailey-girl. Do you hear me? I *need* you to do this. *Please.*" I opened my palm. "Give me your hand."

She eyed my bloody fingers and sucked in a shudder. But she squeezed her eyes shut and slid her hand into mine. I gave her a firm squeeze, as much for my own comfort as hers. My relief at having her here—my Bailey—was so strong, it was crushing. Maybe together we could make it through this.

I placed her palm on my side. "I've got you, Bailey." It was an odd thing to say at a moment like this. It was the only thing to say.

She shook her head and whispered, "I'm sorry." Then she took a breath and leaned in slowly.

I closed my eyes and locked my jaw. Held Bailey's wrist tight, as if doing so would prevent me from being sucked into the blackness again. Pain radiated across my belly and up into my rib cage and deep into my back. I grit my teeth and made myself breathe deep and slow.

I opened my eyes. "Atta girl," I said, trying to keep my voice steady. "Atta girl. Do you have your phone?"

She reached for her hip pocket with her free hand. A little wail escaped her lips. "It's in my backpack."

"Use mine."

Bailey alternately fumbled with the holder on my belt and wiped her nose on the back of her sleeve. I kept a firm hold on her other hand. Now that I had her, I didn't ever want to let her go. She was my own. My granddaughter. And right now, she stood between me and eternity.

One minute, the phone was on my belt, the next, it was in Bailey's hand. I had no memory of the transition. I was blacking out again. No, I couldn't let that happen. I blinked, breathed, tried to concentrate on Bailey's words, spoken into the phone. But they were a blur.

"I don't know… don't know what happened… Please, please, he's bleeding… Oh my God…"

I tried to tell Bailey to let them know we were at the Riviera docks, but my mouth felt like meal. I couldn't speak. Darkness shrouded the corners of my eyes, closing in.

The horrible truth sank in. I'd gambled on the wrong bet. I'd tried to preserve my own life, deceiving myself that I could actually grant Jason's last request. That I could give Bailey a home. But all I'd done was run out of time.

I hadn't told her.

MAILBOAT II

I tried to speak—only to find my body wasn't mine anymore. Wanted nothing to do with me. Had no more use for me. I was looking through a long tunnel, and Bailey and the Mailboat were at the far end. Silence closed over my ears. For a moment, all I could hear was my own heart beating. Slowly. Until that faded away, too.

The last thing I heard was Bailey screaming my name, as if from somewhere far away.

JOIN THE CREW

❋

Ahoy, Shipmate!

If you feel like you're perched on a lighthouse, scanning the horizon for Danielle Lincoln Hanna's next book—good news! You can subscribe to her email newsletter and read a regular ship's log of her writing progress. Better yet, dive deep into the life of the author, hear the scuttlebutt from her personal adventures, spy on her writing process, and catch a rare glimpse of dangerous sea monsters—better known as her pets, Fergus the cat and Angel the German Shepherd.

It's like a message in a bottle washed ashore. All you have to do is open it...

DanielleLincolnHanna.com/newsletter

BOOKS BY DANIELLE LINCOLN HANNA

The Mailboat Suspense Series

Mailboat I: The End of the Pier
Mailboat II: The Silver Helm
Mailboat III: The Captain's Tale
Mailboat IV - *coming summer 2020*

DanielleLincolnHanna.com/shopnow

Pre-order available for Mailboat IV:
DanielleLincolnHanna.com/preorder-mb4

ACKNOWLEDGMENTS

After the release of *Mailboat I: The End of the Pier,* there were a handful of expressions I heard over and over from its devoted readers, especially those who live and vacation in Lake Geneva, Wisconsin. "You got it right" was one of them, and it touches my heart every time I hear it. I feel extremely privileged to write about a town and a lake beloved by so many—especially since this town isn't even my own.

If I got anything right in these first two books of the Mailboat Suspense Series, it's thanks to an army of friends and fans who have helped me along the way.

Once again, my deepest gratitude to the management and staff of the Lake Geneva Cruise Line (www.cruiselakegeneva.com) and the Lake Geneva Mailboat, and specifically to *General Managers Harold Friestad (ret.)* and *Jack Lothian,* to *the Mailboat Captain Neill Frame,* and to *Office Manager Ellen Burling.* Both your help and your blessing have been deeply appreciated.

Thanks also to the many Geneva Lake residents who have made me feel welcome and helped me get to know this special place. *Frank and Jenny Breneisen,* from the day we met, you appointed yourselves my local guides and have not only showered me with your hospitality but have been evangelists-in-chief for the Mailboat Suspense Series. I'm totally in your debt! *Lynda Fergus,* I'm so happy we met through blogging so many years ago. The Coffee Mill will always be our special place! *W. J. Goes and M. Farwell Goes,* you are the two angels behind the scenes, quietly making vital things happen such as the cover art for the series and getting my books into the gift shops at Gage Marine and the Lake Geneva Cruise Line. Margaret, I treasure our conversations under the porch light late into the evening. *Abra Wilkin,* thank you for that first email and for inviting me back to your pier to kiss the goose! You keep my toes in line and push me to be my best.

You know you're doing something right in life when you walk into a police station and the dispatchers simply buzz you through to the staff-only areas. Huge thanks and hugs go to the men and women of the Lake Geneva Police Department. *Lieutenant Edward Gritzner* and *Sergeant Jason Hall,* I literally couldn't write this series without you. Thank you for long hours spent answering completely off-the-wall questions, talking me through fictitious scenarios in all seriousness as if they were real, and reading every word I write for accuracy—not to mention putting up with the rants of an overly perfectionist author. (Few people have brazenly chewed out a police lieutenant, but I have!) *Telecommunicator Rita Moore,* what special moments we've shared, both in and away from the dispatch room. (Keep kicking ass!) *Telecommunicator Courtney Hinzpeter,* thanks for the tour of the police department. *Officer Kara Richardson,* what was meant to be an hour or two ridealong went late into the night. I loved every minute. Thanks for the glimpse into your world and all the cop stories.

Two more individuals round out my team of expert advisers. *Sam Petitto* (retired police officer, Durango, CO), we only talk about once a year, but you're always ready to read my stuff and tear apart any shoddy police work. Thank you! *Dr. Terry Jones,* thanks for walking me through medical questions and scenarios. Your contribution to this series is indispensable. (And you're still the only other person who knows the fate of Tommy. Shhh...)

To my writer's club, *We Write Good,* thank you. You push me to write even gooder. Thank you for all the morbid humor about effing ners, eye-eating goats, crucified kittens, and dozens of other weird-ass things. We're hands-down the best writers club ever. Just sayin'.

My amazing Early Reader Team read Mailboat II prior to publication and provided their comments, critiques, and corrections: *Jennifer Alexander, Kristan Bullinger, Loranda J. Daniels Buoy, Kathy Collins, Brenda Dahlfors, Beth Dancy, Nancy Diestler, Lynda Fergus, Eleanor F.J. Gamarsh, Pat Gerber, Lt. Edward Gritzner, Sgt. Jason Hall, Lynn Hirshman, Dr. Terry Jones, Michelle Bie Love, Lisa McCann, Ellen Mandeville, Steven Maresso, Rebecca Paciorek, Linda Pautz, Sam Petitto, Sanda Putnam, Kimberly Wade, Suzette Titus, Carol D. Westover, Abra Wilkin,* and *Mary-Jane Woodward.* Thanks, crew!

A special thank you to *Maryna Zhukova of MaryDes* (www.MaryDes.eu) for the beautiful cover art. Your creativity, skill, and imagination continue to astound me! Also thanks to my sister *Sandi Hanna Anderson* for staying up late into the night to work a little Photoshop magic while we were supposedly relaxing at a Minnesota lake cabin. The original image of the Mailboat at the pier was a bit of a visual disaster, and you doggedly compared my reference photos to our cover photo and managed to turn out a sharp, tidy image. Hanna Mobile CoWorking gets a five-star review.

Rebecca Paciorek of Blue Dot Marketing (rpaciorek8.wixsite.com/bluedotdigitalmkt), thanks for being my events coordinator. Many of my best memories, connections, and friendships in Lake Geneva happened as a direct result of the tours you wrangled for me.

A little shout-out to *Mark Baumbach* and his friend *Luke Bowman,* the famed duo who ran around Geneva Lake twice in one day, even stopping for a swim, back when they were teenagers in the '70s. "We were looking for some kind of challenge," Mark told me during a chance meeting on Twitter. Mark and his son Maxwell were complaining how Mark and Luke's legendary run is often mentioned, but never credited by name. Well, guys, now it is.

A thousand thanks to you, *my readers.* Bailey, Tommy, Ryan, and Monica's story would merely be words on a page without you. Your imagination brings it to life. Also, thanks for making my dreams come true. I always wanted to be an author.

Finally, snuggles and nose boops to my furkids, *Molly the Adventure Dog* and *Fergus the House Panther.* What is life without a little fur? (Or a lot of fur…) And all my love to *Charles William Maclay,* who recently joined my adventure and made it so much better.

ABOUT THE AUTHOR

Danielle Lincoln Hanna writes Hearth & Homicide Suspense. Equal parts touching and heart-stopping, her writing has been referred to as "cozy thriller." While Danielle now lives in the Rocky Mountains of Montana, her first love is still the Great Plains of North Dakota where she was born. When she's not writing, you can find her hiking with her boyfriend Charles, adventuring with her new puppy Angel, and avoiding surprise attacks from her cat Fergus.

Made in the USA
Las Vegas, NV
27 February 2022

44669866R00111